Love, Lies
& Pina Coladas

By

Zoey Michaels

Table of Contents

Chapter 1: A Comfortable Life —Until It Isn't

Maggie Bennett had everything she was supposed to want. A house with character. A husband who paid the bills on time. A routine that made sense. And yet—

Lately, she felt like she was living inside a house she had already moved out of.

Everything still looked the same. Everything still functioned. But the warmth? The feeling of being home? Gone.

Oliver's keys jingled at the door. Maggie didn't look up from where she sat at the kitchen table, her hands wrapped around a lukewarm mug of tea.

He walked in, tossed his wallet onto the counter, and opened the fridge.

"You already eat?"

She nodded, taking a sip.

"Okay," he said absently.

The fridge door shut. He grabbed a beer, cracked it open, and leaned against the counter.

They used to have long conversations in this kitchen. They used to sit at this very table, talking for hours—about work, about movies, about ridiculous dreams they had no intention of following.

Now? Their house felt like a waiting room. They still functioned like a couple. They just didn't feel like one.

Oliver took a slow pull from his beer, watching Maggie from across the room.

She was right there. But she felt miles away. It hadn't always been like this. They used to have inside jokes. They used to drive home late at night, eating fast food in the car, laughing over nothing.

Now, there was so much silence. So much space between them that he didn't know how to close.

Maggie glanced at Oliver's reflection in the kitchen window. When had they stopped asking each other questions? When had they started filling the space with small talk, instead of actually talking?

When had she started feeling lonely with him right there? The thought was so sharp, so sudden, that she set her mug down too hard.

Oliver glanced up. "Everything okay?"

Maggie forced a smile. "Yeah. Just tired."

But tired wasn't the word. She just didn't know how to say what she really meant. That she missed him. That she missed them.

Chapter 2: Blind Chance

Maggie didn't plan on saying it out loud. Not to Gina. Not to anyone. But the words slipped out anyway.

"Do you ever feel like… you're just going through the motions?"

Gina set down her coffee, eyebrows lifting slightly. "Wow. We're starting with the deep questions today, huh?"

Maggie let out a soft laugh, but it wasn't really funny. Because she wasn't talking about life in general. She was talking about her life.

"You want to elaborate?" Gina prompted.

Maggie hesitated, stirring the foam in her latte.

"It's nothing. I just… I don't know. I feel like Oliver and I are stuck. Like we wake up, go to work, come home, and repeat. And somewhere in all of that, we just… lost something."

Gina studied her.

"Lost what?"

Maggie shook her head. "I don't know. But I miss it."

And that? That was the part that scared her. Because how do you fix something when you don't even know what's broken?

"You're quiet tonight."

Oliver looked up from his beer. Jake was watching him, waiting.

"I'm always quiet," Oliver muttered.

Jake snorted. "Yeah, but this is the 'I'm thinking something and not saying it' kind of quiet."

Oliver exhaled, rubbing a hand over his jaw. "It's nothing."

"Sure." Jake leaned back. "Nothing's why you've been staring at that same spot on the wall for the last ten minutes?"

Oliver sighed. Because Jake wasn't wrong. And if he had been honest, he would have said—

"Do you ever feel like something is missing, but you don't know what?"

But he wasn't honest. Because he didn't want to say those words out loud. So instead, he just shook his head.

"Forget it."

And Jake, thankfully, let it go. For now.

"If you could do anything, what would you do?"

Gina's voice was casual, but Maggie knew better.

"What do you mean?"

"I mean if nothing was stopping you—no responsibilities, no expectations—what would you do?"

Maggie frowned. Because she didn't have an answer. Not anymore. She used to have dreams, plans, ideas. Now, she couldn't remember the last time she had let herself want something just for herself.

Gina nudged her. "Come on, there's got to be something."

Maggie sighed. "I don't know. I just... I want to feel excited about something again."

And the second she said it, she regretted it. Because Gina's eyes gleamed with something dangerous.

"You need to loosen up, man."

Jake's voice was too casual.

Oliver shot him a look. "And what's that supposed to mean?"

"It means you've been living the same day for years."

Oliver took a slow sip of his beer. "That's called stability."

"That's called boring."

Oliver rolled his eyes. "Not all of us want to live like you."

"Oh, I know. But you used to want more than this. You used to have fun."

Oliver didn't answer. Because Jake wasn't wrong. But admitting that? Wasn't an option.

"I did something," Gina said later, far too casually.

Maggie narrowed her eyes. "Gina..."

"Relax, it's not bad."

"That's exactly what someone says before revealing something bad."

Gina grinned. "Fine. I made you a profile."

Maggie blinked. "You did what?"

"Oh, don't look at me like that. I didn't use your real name. It's just an experiment."

Maggie groaned. "Tell me you didn't put my face on some sketchy dating site."

"Of course not! It's just a conversation starter." Gina waved a hand. "You don't even have to check it. I was just curious what kind of people would respond."

"You were curious?" Maggie said flatly.

"Yep." Gina took a sip of her drink.

Maggie glared.

Then—her phone buzzed.

And for some reason, she didn't look away.

"You know, this kinda sounds like you."

Jake slid his phone across the table.

Oliver frowned. "What is this?"

"Something I came across."

"You're on those sites?" Oliver smirked.

"Not for me. But I see things."

Oliver rolled his eyes.

Then, just to humor him—he read the message. And froze. Because something about it felt familiar. He didn't know why. But suddenly, he couldn't stop reading.

Chapter 3: Familiar Strangers

Maggie shouldn't have looked. She had told herself she wouldn't.

But later that night, while curled up on the couch, her thumb hovered over the notification Gina had so smugly left on her phone.

One new message. It was probably some stranger saying something ridiculous. Probably nothing. But still…

She hesitated. Then, before she could second-guess herself—she tapped it open. The message was simple.

Him: If you could go anywhere right now, where would it be?

Maggie frowned. No "Hey." No weird pickup lines. Just… a question. A *real* question. Without thinking too much, she typed back.

Her: Anywhere with good music and a strong drink. You?

A pause. Then—

Him: Anywhere that doesn't feel like the same day on repeat.

And just like that—something stirred inside her. Because she knew *exactly* what he meant.

Oliver had meant to ignore it. Jake had shown him the profile as a joke. And at first, that's all it was.

But now, sitting alone in his truck, parked outside the house he wasn't ready to go into yet, he found himself pulling up the message again.

He didn't know why. It was stupid. Pointless. But instead of closing it, he typed.

Him: If you could go anywhere right now, where would it be?

And then—he waited. Even though he told himself he didn't care. Even though he told himself he wouldn't check.

But when his phone buzzed—he checked. And something about her answer made his chest tighten. Because suddenly, it didn't feel like talking to a stranger. It felt like talking to someone he already knew.

Neither of them expected to keep replying. Neither of them expected it to be... easy. But somehow, the messages kept coming.

Her: What's the worst vacation you've ever taken?

Him: Ever been to a beach resort during a storm? Nothing like paying for ocean views you can't see.

Her: So you're saying you don't like surprises?

Him: Depends on the surprise.

A pause. Then—

Her: What about this?

Oliver stared at the words longer than necessary. Then, before he could overthink it—

Him: Still deciding.

Maggie shouldn't be smiling. But she was. It wasn't even flirty. It was just... fun. It felt easy. And she hadn't felt easy in a long time.

She started checking for messages without meaning to. Started wondering what he'd say next. Started catching herself waiting for the next response.

And that? That was when she knew—this wasn't nothing anymore.

Oliver caught himself pulling out his phone too fast. Caught himself thinking about responses during the day.

And one night, when Maggie sat across from him at the dinner table, staring at her plate in silence, pushing food around with her fork...

He felt it sink in. That whatever this was—it wasn't just an escape anymore. Because if it were, he wouldn't feel guilty.

And yet—he didn't stop. Not yet.

Chapter 4: Dangerous Conversations

Maggie told herself it was just conversation. That's it. Nothing more. She wasn't flirting. She wasn't crossing a line. She was just... talking.

But then, why did she check her phone first thing in the morning? Why did she catch herself waiting for a response? Why did it feel like something was waking up inside her that had been asleep for a long time?

Oliver told himself he could stop whenever he wanted. That it was nothing serious. Nothing dangerous. And yet—

The messages had started feeling familiar. Like inside jokes. Like conversations that flowed too easily. Like something he wasn't ready to name. And that? That should have been his first warning.

Her: What's something you used to love that you forgot about?

Oliver hesitated. It was a simple question. An easy one. And yet, his chest tightened. Because the first thing that came to mind wasn't a thing. It was a *person*. And suddenly, he couldn't type the truth. So instead, he sent—

Him: Sunday mornings. The kind where you wake up late and don't have anywhere to be.

The response came faster than he expected.

Her: That sounds nice. I haven't had one of those in a long time.

Oliver stared at the words. Because somehow, that felt true for him too.

"You're smiling at your phone."

Maggie nearly dropped it. "What?"

Gina smirked, sipping her coffee. "You heard me. You've got that look."

"I don't have a look."

"Maggie. Please. You've had that look since high school. Who is he?"

Maggie's stomach twisted.

"No one."

Gina raised an eyebrow.

Maggie swallowed hard. "It's just... conversation."

"Mmmhmm." Gina leaned forward. "So, when are you meeting him?"

Maggie froze.

"I'm not."

Gina shrugged. "Okay."

Maggie exhaled.

Then—

"But if you were..." Gina's grin was teasing. "Where would it be?"

Maggie didn't answer. Because the truth was—she didn't know anymore.

"You're acting weird."

Oliver looked up.

Jake was watching him over the pool table, expression unreadable.

"What are you talking about?" Oliver said.

"You've been checking your phone every five minutes."

Oliver rolled his eyes. "I have not."

"Yeah? You're doing it right now."

Oliver glanced down—his phone was in his hand.

Jake let out a low whistle. "Man, you've got it bad."

Oliver frowned.

"It's just conversation."

Jake smirked. "Sure. Let me know when you start believing that."

And the worst part?

Jake wasn't wrong.

Maggie stared at her screen for a long time. Her heart pounded. Because this?

This was the moment she should stop. This was the moment to walk away. But instead, she typed—

Her: Do you ever wonder if things could have gone differently?

She held her breath. Then, after a long pause—

Him: Yeah.

And just like that—

They both knew they weren't going to stop. Not yet. Not when it felt like they had just started.

Chapter 5: Unnamed Choices

Maggie knew she should stop. She had already crossed the line. Not physically. Not yet. But emotionally? She had stepped over it days ago. And the worst part? She didn't want to turn back.

Oliver wasn't an idiot. He knew what this was. Knew that if he had to hide it, it wasn't innocent. And yet—

Every time he thought about stopping, his chest felt tight. Like there was something unfinished. Like there was a version of himself that he wasn't ready to let go of yet. And so—he kept going.

Her: If you could drop everything and go get a drink right now, where would it be?

Oliver stared at the message. He should ignore it. Should shut this down. But instead, he typed—

Him: Somewhere quiet. Good drinks. No expectations.

A pause. Then—

Her: That sounds nice.

Oliver hesitated. Then, before he could stop himself—

Him: If we were in the same place, I'd say we test that theory.

Maggie felt the weight of it. She should say no. She should delete the app. She should walk away. But her fingers hovered over the keyboard. Because this wasn't about meeting a stranger.

It was about feeling something again. And wasn't that what she had wanted? To feel something other than empty? So she did the only thing she could think of.

Her: Ask me again tomorrow.

Because if she was going to take a risk—she needed to be sure.

Oliver stared at the screen. A part of him felt relieved. Because now, he had an out. A way to stop this before it was too late.

But instead of walking away— He waited. Because deep down, he knew. Tomorrow *would* come. And he'd still want to ask.

Chapter 6: The Lingering Question

Maggie had told herself she wouldn't think about it. She had promised herself that today would feel normal. But it wasn't. Because the question still sat there. Waiting. Looming. And she wasn't sure if she wanted to say no.

Oliver woke up knowing today was different. Because it was the day he was supposed to ask again. And the worst part?

He wanted to. Even though it was reckless. Even though it was wrong. Even though a part of him knew that once he asked, there would be no going back.

Maggie's phone buzzed while she was brushing her hair. She knew what it was before she even looked. Her fingers hesitated over the screen. Then, finally—she opened it.

Him: So, is today the day?

Her breath caught. Because this? This was the moment. The line in the sand. The yes or no that would change everything.

Her hands felt unsteady. Because she could still walk away. She could still pretend none of this had ever happened. But instead— She typed:

Her: What if it is?

And hit send.

The second her message came through, Oliver's stomach tightened. Because now—it was real.

No more pretending this was just a hypothetical. No more hiding behind half-answers.

This was happening. And suddenly, he felt something between fear and relief. Because he didn't want to stop. So before he could second-guess himself—he responded.

Him: Then I guess we're about to find out.

Maggie sat on the edge of the bed, staring at the message. Her hands were clammy. Her heart was racing.

And for the first time since this all started—she felt afraid. Not because of Oliver. But because of what this meant. Because the second she walked out that door—she couldn't take it back.

She swallowed hard. Then, with a slow exhale—she stood up. And got ready to leave.

Chapter 7: Crossing Lines

Maggie shouldn't be here. She knew that the second she stepped inside. The second the familiar scent of lime and salt hit her. The second she saw the same worn leather barstools, the same dim neon glow.

This wasn't just a bar. It was *their* bar. And now, she was here. Waiting for someone who **wasn't** Oliver.

She should leave, she thought. She hadn't ordered yet. Hadn't even taken off her coat. Because the longer she sat there, the more this started to feel like a mistake.

A bad idea. A terrible, horrible, no-good idea. Her stomach twisted. What was she thinking? She wasn't ready for this. She should leave. **Now.** *Before it was too late.* She reached for her purse. She was already halfway out of her seat when—

The door swung open. And everything stopped. Because standing there— Right there, in the doorway—Was Oliver.

Her breath caught. Her stomach dropped. And in an instant—she knew. She knew before he saw her. Before his eyes met hers. Before the shock flashed across his face like a slow-motion car crash.

Because suddenly, it wasn't a mystery anymore. Suddenly—this was real. He had been looking for someone else. Not Maggie. Not his wife.

And yet—there she was. Sitting at the bar. Looking at him like she had just seen a ghost. And maybe that's what this was.

A ghost of everything they used to be. Of everything they had forgotten. Of everything they had lost.

His pulse pounded in his ears. Because suddenly, everything about this—made sense. And suddenly, none of it did.

Maggie moved first. She had two choices. Sit back down or walk out the door. Her legs chose the second. But before she could make it past him—

"Maggie."

Her name wasn't a question. It wasn't even a statement. It was a collision. And it made her stop. For a second, neither of them moved. Neither of them spoke. They just stood there.

Maggie could hear the hum of conversation behind them. The clink of glasses. The lazy strum of a guitar from the jukebox. But between them? Silence. Heavy. Tangled. Unfinished. Then, finally—

"What are you doing here?"

She didn't know if she said it first. Or if he did. Or if it even mattered. Because now, they were here. And there was no walking away from it.

Chapter 8: No Moral High Ground

Maggie could feel the heat rising in her face, and it had nothing to do with the tequila sitting untouched in front of her.

Across from her, Oliver leaned on the bar, his fingers wrapped tight around his own shot glass. His jaw was locked, his breathing steady, but his eyes—his eyes were sharp. Unreadable.

Neither of them spoke for a long, stretched-out moment. Because what was there to say? They had both been here to meet someone else.

There was no moral high ground. No righteous anger that didn't come laced with hypocrisy. Maggie exhaled slowly, trying to collect her thoughts, but Oliver got there first.

"So, what?" he asked, voice carefully neutral. "Were you planning on going through with it?"

Maggie bristled. "I don't know, Oliver. Were you?"

His lips pressed into a thin line.

That's what she thought.

They both turned back to their drinks, avoiding each other's gaze.

Then, Oliver scoffed under his breath and shook his head. "How long have you been doing this?"

Maggie blinked. "What?"

He turned to her fully now, leaning against the bar, arms crossed. "How long have you been going behind my back, Maggie?"

A sharp pang of indignation shot through her. "Excuse me?"

Oliver's expression darkened. "I mean, it can't be a coincidence that we both ended up here tonight. That's… convenient."

Maggie let out a short, humorless laugh. "Oh, so now I'm some kind of serial cheater? That's rich, Oliver."

"You tell me." His voice was clipped. "Because I just walked in here to meet someone I thought was a stranger, only to find out my wife is sitting at the bar looking like she just got caught."

Maggie's fingers curled into fists at her sides. "Oh, and you were just here to grab a drink, right? That's it?"

He exhaled sharply. "No, Maggie. I was here because Jake saw a profile and thought I should respond. And since we're both throwing accusations around, how long were you planning on keeping your little secret?"

"Oh, for—" Maggie groaned and raked a hand through her hair. "I didn't even make the profile, Oliver! Gina set it up without telling me!"

That made him pause.

She let out a breath, arms folded tight across her chest. "Yeah. That's right. Gina. Who didn't know it would be you responding."

Oliver stared at her, processing.

Then, to her utter frustration, he laughed.

Maggie scowled. "What now?"

Oliver ran a hand over his jaw, shaking his head. "Jake saw the profile and told me to answer."

Maggie blinked.

Her mind worked through the pieces at lightning speed. Gina had made the profile. Jake had seen it. Neither had known about the other. And somehow, that had led them here.

Maggie's shoulders dropped. "Oh, you have got to be kidding me."

Oliver just kept laughing, shaking his head. "Nope."

She groaned, dropping her face into her hands. "We are never going to live this down."

Lupe, who had been watching them with open amusement, finally let out a low chuckle. "Oh, I don't know. I think this might be the best thing to happen to you two in a while."

Maggie shot him a glare. "Not the time, Lupe."

Oliver, still chuckling under his breath, reached for the second shot that Lupe had poured earlier and tipped it toward Maggie before drinking it down.

She huffed. "You're handling this a little too well."

"Are you kidding?" Oliver set his empty glass down and smirked. "This is the most ridiculous thing that's ever happened to me. Of course, I'm laughing."

Maggie exhaled sharply and shook her head. "So what now?"

Lupe folded her arms, grinning. "Now you do the only thing that makes sense."

Maggie frowned. "Which is?"

"One week." Lupe leaned forward. "Give yourselves one week. You clearly didn't plan for this—so maybe the universe did."

Oliver raised a brow. "The universe?"

Lupe shrugged. "Or Gina and Jake. Either way, somebody is clearly giving you a chance here."

Maggie snorted. "A chance for what?"

"To figure out if there's anything left worth saving," Lupe said simply.

The words shouldn't have landed so hard.

But they did.

Maggie glanced at Oliver. He was already watching her.

She swallowed. One week.

She could already hear Gina in her head. What's the worst that could happen?

Maggie exhaled.

Fine.

She turned back to Lupe, shaking her head. "One week."

Oliver watched her for a beat longer. Then, finally—he nodded.

"One week."

And just like that—everything changed.

Chapter 9: One Week Starts Now

The air outside the bar was cool, crisp. It should have cleared Maggie's head. Should have helped her breathe.

It didn't.

Oliver stood a few steps away, hands in his pockets, eyes trained on the pavement like he was still trying to process what just happened.

Maggie wasn't doing much better.

They had just agreed—somehow—to one week. What had she been thinking?

She wrapped her arms around herself, exhaling slowly. "Well. That was unexpected."

Oliver let out a quiet scoff. "You think?"

Silence.

The weight of it pressed between them, thick and unsteady.

Maggie glanced over. Oliver's brow was furrowed, his mouth set in a tight line. He was deep in thought, probably questioning everything—same as her.

She shifted her weight. "So... we're really doing this?"

Oliver finally looked at her. "I guess we are."

A long beat passed.

Then, a little dryly, Oliver added, "Unless you want to bail."

Maggie let out a soft laugh—one she hadn't expected. "And admit Lupe was right? Not a chance."

Oliver huffed, something close to amusement flickering over his face. "Figured."

Another pause.

Then Oliver glanced toward the parking lot. "You driving?"

Maggie hesitated. The idea of getting in a car with him, going back to the same house, pretending like they could just... coexist again for a week—

It was overwhelming.

But she had agreed.

So she nodded. "Yeah. I'll drive."

Oliver followed her to the car.

She didn't miss the way his steps hesitated before getting in. She wasn't sure if it made her feel better or worse that he looked just as unsure as she felt.

The hum of the engine filled the silence. Maggie gripped the wheel a little tighter than necessary, her focus locked on the road.

She wasn't sure what to say. Every topic that popped into her head felt too loaded, too delicate, too dangerous. But apparently, Oliver didn't share that hesitation.

"So." He cleared his throat. "Ground rules?"

Maggie snuck a glance at him. "Ground rules?"

He nodded, eyes on the windshield. "We live together for a week. We don't have to pretend everything's normal, but we do have to survive it."

Maggie smirked. "Ambitious."

Oliver shot her a look. "You got a better idea?"

She thought for a second. "No yelling."

Oliver snorted. "Can't promise that."

Maggie sighed. "Fine. Minimal yelling."

Oliver nodded. "Fair."

She tapped her fingers against her knee. "No bringing up the past just to win an argument."

Oliver hesitated. Then sighed. "Alright."

Maggie lifted a finger. "And no physical contact."

At that, Oliver actually laughed.

Maggie scowled. "What?"

He smirked, shaking his head. "Nothing."

She narrowed her eyes. "You think this is funny?"

Oliver shrugged, still smirking. "You were literally about to go on a date with some stranger tonight, and now you're worried about what? Accidentally brushing my hand when we reach for the remote?"

Maggie's face heated. "That's not—"

But he wasn't wrong.

She huffed. "Whatever. It's a rule."

Oliver held up his hands in surrender. "No touching. Got it."

Maggie settled back into her seat, staring at the road ahead.

One week.

They could do this.

Right?

The house felt different.

Not physically—everything was exactly where it had been when she left earlier. But now, there was a weight in the air that wasn't there before.

Oliver tossed his keys on the counter and turned to her. "You want the bed or the guest room?"

Maggie blinked. "I—I don't care."

Oliver arched a brow. "You sure?"

Maggie hesitated. She wasn't sure. But the idea of making a decision suddenly felt overwhelming.

She waved a hand. "It's fine. Do whatever."

Oliver studied her for a second longer, then nodded. "Alright. I'll take the guest room."

Maggie exhaled. She should be relieved. Instead, she just felt off. She moved toward the hallway, but Oliver's voice stopped her.

"Hey, Maggie."

She turned. He was leaning against the counter, arms crossed. For a second, he almost looked like the Oliver she used to know.

His gaze was steady. "It's just a week. We can handle that, right?"

Maggie swallowed. Nodded. "Yeah."

She wasn't sure if she believed it. But she said it anyway. Then, before she could overthink it, she turned and walked to the bedroom.

Late that night Maggie lay awake, staring at the ceiling. The bed felt too big. The silence too loud.

She turned over, trying to shut off her brain. But sleep didn't come easy. Not tonight. Not with Oliver just down the hall.

Chapter 10: The First Morning

Maggie woke up groggy, her mind sluggish with the weight of the night before.

For a second, she forgot. Forgot where she was. Forgot why her stomach felt tight. Forgot why there was an unsettling quiet in the house.

Then it all came back. The bar. Oliver. One week.

She exhaled slowly, staring at the ceiling. The bed felt too big. The room felt too empty. Which was ridiculous, because this was her bed. She had been sleeping alone for months. But today? Today, it felt different.

She rolled onto her side, catching sight of the soft morning light creeping in through the curtains. Then she heard it. Footsteps.

For a split second, her half-asleep brain panicked. Then she remembered—Oliver.

Maggie closed her eyes briefly, steeling herself before pushing back the covers and sitting up.

Just a week, she reminded herself. You can survive this.

By the time Maggie made her way down the hall, the smell of coffee was already thick in the air. For a ridiculous moment, she hesitated at the doorway.

Then, she saw him. Oliver stood at the counter, mug in hand, leaning slightly against the island like he had done a thousand times before. But this time? This time, it felt foreign. Like he was an old habit she wasn't sure how to pick up again.

Oliver turned his head at the sound of her footsteps. Their eyes met. Maggie didn't know what to say. Neither, apparently, did Oliver. He just lifted his mug in a silent greeting before taking another sip.

Maggie exhaled, moving to the cabinet. She reached for a mug, trying not to notice the way Oliver's presence made the kitchen feel smaller.

"Didn't know if you still drank it the same way," Oliver finally said, nodding toward the pot.

Maggie hesitated. "I do."

He didn't say anything else.

She poured herself a cup, avoiding looking at him too long. It shouldn't feel this strange. But it did.

Maggie wrapped her hands around the warm ceramic, grasping for something normal. Something easy.

"So..." she started, voice a little too light, "I guess this is the part where we figure out how this works."

Oliver smirked slightly, tilting his head. "You mean coexisting?"

Maggie raised an eyebrow. "I was going to say not killing each other, but sure."

Oliver's lips twitched, like he was fighting a real smile. "Sounds like a solid plan."

A small, fleeting moment of levity passed between them. Then, just as quickly, it disappeared. Because neither of them knew what came next.

Oliver cleared his throat. "I, uh… hope you don't mind. I grabbed some of my stuff from the guest room closet."

Maggie blinked. "I don't mind."

She hadn't even thought about that. The guest room had always been half his anyway. A place for his random things, spare clothes, the things he never got around to organizing. The thought sent a strange feeling through her.

She took a slow sip of her coffee. "Did you sleep okay?"

Oliver hesitated. "Yeah."

Maggie wasn't sure if she believed him. Because she sure hadn't.

The silence settled between them again. It wasn't hostile. Just hesitant. Like two people standing at the edge of something they weren't sure they wanted to cross.

Maggie cleared her throat. "What's on your schedule today?"

Oliver shrugged. "Meetings. A site visit in the afternoon."

Maggie nodded, stirring her coffee absently. "I have a project deadline. Probably won't come up for air until later."

Oliver smirked. "Sounds about right."

She looked up. "What's that supposed to mean?"

His smirk grew. "Just that you get weird when you're in work mode."

Maggie rolled her eyes, but a tiny part of her almost smiled. Because that was familiar. That was the way they used to talk. But before she could hold onto it, Oliver shifted, adjusting his watch.

"I should get going," he said.

Maggie nodded. "Right. Me too."

Neither of them moved right away. Then Oliver reached for his keys and walked toward the door.

Maggie stood there, still holding her coffee, watching him leave the way she had watched him leave so many times before.

But this time—this time, she wasn't sure how she felt about it.

Chapter 11: Old Patterns, New Tension

Maggie sat at her desk, fingers hovering over her keyboard, but her mind wasn't on her work. Which was ridiculous. She had deadlines. Emails to send. Clients waiting for updates.

And yet— Her thoughts kept drifting. Back to the kitchen. Back to Oliver. Back to how normal it had felt for a second—before it didn't.

She exhaled sharply, pushing her chair back and standing up. Pacing usually helped when her mind wouldn't focus.

She had been through difficult seasons before. Stress. Distractions. Losing herself in work. But nothing—nothing—had ever felt quite like this.

One week. It had felt like a reasonable timeframe last night. Like something manageable. But sitting here now? One week felt like a lifetime.

Across town, Oliver leaned against the hood of his truck, watching his team finalize the structural inspection on the latest project site.

But his head wasn't in it. He barely heard the conversation happening a few feet away. Because his mind was stuck in his kitchen. On the way Maggie had lingered before speaking.

On the way she had looked at him when she thought he wasn't paying attention. On the fact that it was way too easy to fall into old rhythms with her.

And that? That was dangerous.

Oliver had thought this would be simple. One week of forced proximity, awkward conversations, then they'd go their separate ways.

But now? Now, he wasn't so sure.

Maggie finally gave up on being productive around noon. Her stomach rumbled, pulling her toward the kitchen. But the second she stepped in—she hesitated.

Because on the counter, right next to her laptop, was a takeout bag. She frowned. That wasn't there earlier. Stepping closer, she saw a note scribbled on the outside.

Figured you'd forget to eat. Don't be weird about it. —O

Maggie blinked. Her stomach twisted—but not from hunger.

She had lost count of how many times Oliver had done this over the years. Bringing her food when she got too buried in work to think about meals.

She used to tease him about it. Used to roll her eyes and call him overprotective. Used to act like she didn't love it.

But now? Now, she didn't know how to feel. Because it meant he still knew her. Still thought about her. And maybe—just maybe—that made things more complicated.

Oliver sat in his truck, parked outside his next site visit, but he hadn't moved yet. Because he knew Maggie had probably seen the food by now.

And he didn't know if that had been a mistake. He hadn't planned to do it. Hadn't planned anything, really. But stopping by her favorite café on his way into town? That had been instinct. Because this was what he did. And maybe—just maybe—that was the problem.

Maggie hadn't seen Oliver since this morning, and she wasn't sure if that was good or bad. But when he finally walked through the door, she felt the air shift.

Oliver set his keys down, glancing toward her. "Hey."

Maggie hesitated. Then—before she could talk herself out of it—she lifted the empty takeout bag.

Oliver's expression didn't change. "You ate."

It wasn't a question.

Maggie nodded slowly. "Yeah."

A pause.

Then, softer—"Thank you."

Oliver's brow lifted slightly, like he hadn't expected her to acknowledge it.

He just nodded once. "No problem."

Silence.

The weight of everything unspoken sat heavy between them. And for the first time, Maggie wondered— If one week would be enough to figure this out.

Chapter 12: Old Habits, New Awareness

Maggie wasn't sure what she expected when Oliver came home that evening, but she wasn't expecting things to feel...

Normal. Not completely. But enough that it threw her off. Because despite everything, they still functioned like two people who had lived together for years.

She knew how he took his coffee. He knew that she liked silence in the morning. She knew that he left his keys on the counter. He knew she worked late and would forget to eat.

The mechanics of their life together had never been the problem. The problem was everything else.

Maggie was standing at the sink, rinsing out her mug, when Oliver walked past on his way to the fridge.

It was nothing. A simple moment. A routine interaction. But when she turned slightly, Oliver was closer than she expected.

Close enough that his arm brushed hers as he reached for a bottle of water. Close enough that she caught the familiar scent of his cologne.

Close enough that, for one breathless second, her body remembered what it felt like to be near him.

Maggie stilled. So did Oliver. It wasn't dramatic. Just a shift. Like the kind you feel when a storm is about to roll in.

Their eyes met. And it hit her—hard. This was the longest they had been this close since the bar.

Neither of them moved. Neither of them spoke. But something was very, very different.

Maggie was the first to step back. Too fast, too sharp—like she'd touched something hot.

Oliver noticed. But he didn't call her out on it. He just took his water and leaned against the counter, watching her.

Maggie turned to grab a towel, drying her hands with far too much focus.

"Long day?" she asked, voice a little too casually.

Oliver tilted his head slightly. "You don't have to do that."

Maggie blinked. "Do what?"

"Fill the space."

Her grip on the towel tightened. He wasn't wrong. She hated the silence. Because silence meant thinking. And thinking meant feeling.

And feeling? That was the one thing she wasn't ready for.

Oliver pushed off the counter, heading toward the hallway. "I'm grabbing a shower."

Maggie nodded, relieved for the exit. "Okay."

But then— He paused. Turned back slightly. And without looking directly at her, he said, "You wanna grab dinner later?"

Maggie's heart skipped a beat. Not because of the question itself. But because of the way he said it.

Like it was normal. Like they weren't whatever this was. Like this wasn't dangerous territory.

Maggie hesitated. "Dinner?"

Oliver nodded. "Yeah." He shrugged. "Figured we have to eat."

She studied him carefully. This isn't a date, she told herself. This is just… logistical. But then—why did it feel like something more?

She swallowed hard. "Okay."

Oliver held her gaze for a second longer.

Then nodded once before disappearing down the hall. And Maggie stood there, gripping the counter, trying to steady herself. Because this thing between them? It was growing. And she wasn't sure if she was ready for it.

Chapter 13: Dinner and Everything Left Unsaid

Maggie almost backed out. She had plenty of reasons—work, exhaustion, the fact that spending too much time with Oliver felt like walking a tightrope with no safety net. But she had agreed.

And Oliver? He didn't bring it up again. Didn't remind her. Didn't push. Which somehow made it worse. Because now, if she bailed, she'd be the one making it weird. So she went.

The Restaurant wasn't fancy. Just a little family-owned place they used to go to before. Back when date nights were a thing. Back when they still tried.

Oliver didn't say anything when they walked in, but Maggie saw the way his eyes flickered with recognition. She almost asked if he had done it on purpose. But then he pulled out a chair for her, and for some reason, the question stuck in her throat.

The first few minutes were fine. Easy, even.

They talked about work. The weather. Gina and Jake's absurd matchmaking skills. For a little while, it almost felt... comfortable. Until it didn't.

Because underneath all of it—there was an undercurrent. A heaviness. The kind that came from knowing someone too well. The kind that came from knowing exactly what wasn't being said.

Maggie was pushing food around on her plate when Oliver spoke.

"So." He cleared his throat. "This week… is it as weird for you as it is for me?"

Maggie froze. She hadn't expected him to acknowledge it.

She hesitated. "What do you mean?"

Oliver leaned back slightly, watching her. "I mean…" He exhaled, rubbing his jaw. "We've been circling each other like strangers. But we're not."

Maggie swallowed. "I know."

Oliver's gaze was steady. "Then why does it feel like we are?"

She didn't have an answer. Not one she was willing to say out loud.

Oliver sighed, setting his fork down. "I don't know how we got here, Mags."

The nickname hit her like a punch to the stomach. Because it was effortless. Like it had never gone away.

Maggie inhaled sharply, pushing back the sudden wave of emotion. "Yeah. Me neither."

Oliver studied her. For a second, she thought he was going to press. To say something real. But then—he didn't.

He just gave a small, tired nod. "Guess we'll figure it out."

And Maggie didn't know if she wanted to. Because figuring it out meant facing it. And facing it meant acknowledging everything they had lost.

Silence filled the car on the drive back home. Not cold. Not angry. Just full. Full of everything that had almost been said. Full of everything neither of them was ready to admit.

And as they pulled into the driveway, Maggie had never felt so aware of the distance between them.

Because for all their history— Right now, Oliver felt further away than ever.

Chapter 14: The Unexpected Shift

The house was quiet when they got back. Too quiet. Not the kind of peaceful silence that felt like comfort. The kind that felt like something waiting to happen.

Maggie dropped her purse onto the entryway table and toed off her shoes. Oliver locked the door behind them. "You want the TV on?"

It was a simple question. But Maggie hesitated. Because the idea of background noise felt safer. Like a buffer between them and whatever this thing was building between them.

She nodded. "Yeah. Sure."

Oliver turned toward the living room, flipping on the screen as he walked past the couch. And just like that, they fell into old habits.

She went to the kitchen for water. He sat down, flipping channels mindlessly. She lingered, debating whether to go straight to bed or—

She didn't know what. But then—it happened. Maggie had only meant to grab a glass. That was it. But as she reached up, fingers brushing the rim of the cup, her balance shifted slightly. And before she could correct herself—she wobbled. Not a lot. Just enough.

Just enough that the glass slipped from her grasp, tumbling forward— And before she could react—Oliver was already there. Not thinking. Just moving.

His hands caught her waist, steadying her before she could even stumble back. The glass? It landed safely in the sink, rolling to a stop.

But Maggie was still frozen. Because Oliver's hands were still there. Familiar. Warm. Holding her like muscle memory. Like he had done a hundred times before. But this time—it felt different.

Maggie turned slowly, her breath shallow. Oliver didn't move. His hands were still resting against her waist—like he wasn't sure if he should let go yet. Their eyes met.

And in that moment—everything changed. Because suddenly— there was no space between them. No sarcasm. No tension. No distance. Just awareness.

Maggie should step back. She should say something. But instead—she just stood there. Because her body wasn't listening to logic right now.

Because Oliver wasn't looking at her like a stranger. He was looking at her like he used to. Like she was someone he had spent years memorizing.

Like she was someone he hadn't forgotten how to hold. And for one second—one breath—one heartbeat—she let herself feel it.

Oliver exhaled slowly. His hands flexed slightly, like he was about to step back— But then— Maggie's fingers twitched. Not much.

Just enough that her hands brushed against his forearms. A small, unconscious movement. But Oliver felt it.

She knew he did. Because his whole body tensed. Because his breath hitched just slightly. Because for the first time in forever—neither of them wanted to move.

And for one reckless, impossible second—Maggie wondered. What if she didn't pull away? What if she just— But then—the moment shattered.

Oliver's hands dropped first. The warmth of his touch disappeared like it had never been there at all. Maggie felt the loss instantly. She stepped back, clearing her throat. "Uh… thanks."

Oliver nodded once, looking at the floor. "Yeah. No problem."

The air was thick. Suffocating. Like they had just crossed a line without meaning to. Like they had just come dangerously close to something neither of them was ready for.

Maggie grabbed the glass, filling it with water to keep her hands busy.

Oliver took a step back. "I should—" He gestured vaguely toward the hallway. "I should call it a night."

Maggie nodded, too quickly. "Right. Me too."

Silence.

Oliver turned slightly, taking a step toward the guest room. Then—he paused.

Over his shoulder, voice dry but with the faintest hint of something else—something softer—he muttered,

"Careful, Hazard."

Maggie froze. Her stomach twisted at the familiarity of it. At the way it rolled off his tongue so easily. Like no time had passed at all.

She gripped the counter a little tighter. "Shut up, Oliver."

His chuckle was quiet. Almost fond. And then—he was gone. Leaving Maggie alone in the kitchen. Leaving her with a racing pulse and a truth she wasn't ready to admit.

That for the first time in forever— She didn't want to stop feeling him.

Chapter 15: A Line That Won't Stay Crossed

Maggie told herself it was nothing. A reaction. A habit. Oliver had steadied her because that's what people did when someone almost knocked over a glass.

And calling her Hazard? That was just muscle memory. A joke. A leftover piece of their past that didn't mean anything.

But her body wasn't buying it. Because she could still feel his hands. Still hear the quiet chuckle in his voice. Still feel the way her heart had tripped over itself when he said it.

Maggie clenched her jaw and flipped onto her side, yanking the blankets up to her chin. It was nothing. It had to be nothing. Because if it was anything more? She didn't know what she was supposed to do with that.

Maggie woke up with one goal. To act normal. Like last night hadn't happened. Like she hadn't spent the last two hours lying awake, staring at the ceiling, replaying every second of it.

She rolled out of bed, threw on a sweater, and went to the kitchen—prepared for awkwardness. What she wasn't prepared for was the smell of coffee already brewing.

Maggie slowed. That was new. Oliver never made coffee first. But there he was, standing at the counter, pouring a fresh cup like it was just another Tuesday morning. Like this was normal.

Maggie hesitated in the doorway. "You made coffee?"

Oliver didn't look up. "Figured you'd need it."

She blinked. "You don't even drink it this early."

Oliver shrugged. "Guess I do now."

Maggie narrowed her eyes. Because this? This wasn't normal. Not anymore. Not since everything had gone off the rails.

And yet—here he was. Making her coffee. Not just existing in the same space, but participating. And Maggie didn't know what to do with that.

Maggie sat at the table, fingers curled around her mug, trying not to let her brain turn this into something bigger than it was.

"So," she said, aiming for casual, "any big plans today?"

Oliver leaned against the counter, sipping his water. "Meetings."

Maggie hummed. "Same."

A beat. Silence. Then—

"You okay?" Oliver asked, brows slightly raised.

Maggie froze. "What?"

"You're acting weird."

She almost choked on her coffee. "I'm not acting weird."

Oliver just stared. That flat, unimpressed stare he always used to give her when she was lying.

Maggie huffed. "I'm not."

Oliver smirked, sipping his water. "Whatever you say, Hazard."

Maggie gripped the table a little too hard. Because there it was again. That darn nickname. Like he was testing her. Or worse— he wasn't.

Maybe he just didn't realize what it did to her. Or maybe he did. Either way, Maggie needed out of this conversation. So she pushed back from the table, too quickly. "I should get to work."

Oliver lifted a brow but didn't argue. "Right."

Maggie took her coffee and all but fled to her office, heart racing for no reason at all. Because this wasn't supposed to happen. She was supposed to get through this week, not start feeling things.

But Oliver was making it really hard to forget why she had fallen for him in the first place.

Oliver knew exactly what he was doing. He knew Maggie was spooked. Knew last night had shaken her more than she wanted to admit. And maybe—*just maybe*—that's why he wasn't pretending anymore.

Because last night? That was something. Whether she wanted to admit it or not. So, yeah. He had made coffee. And, yeah. He had called her Hazard. And maybe, just maybe—he'd keep doing things like that.

Because Maggie wasn't the only one struggling with this. And if he had to suffer through it, then so did she.

By the time evening rolled around, Maggie had done everything possible to avoid thinking about Oliver. She had drowned herself in work. Blasted music while cleaning. Even made an excuse to leave the house for an hour.

But life had other plans. Because when she walked into the kitchen to grab a snack— Oliver was already there. Leaning against the counter. Looking too comfortable. Like this was still his house. Which, technically—it was.

Maggie hesitated. "You need the kitchen?"

Oliver lifted a brow. "It's a kitchen, Maggie. It fits two people."

She scowled. Maggie ignored him and went to the fridge, reaching for the leftover takeout container—

Only for Oliver to reach at the same time. Their hands brushed. Both of them froze. And suddenly, it was like last night all over again. The charged air. The pause in movement. The heavy, undeniable awareness.

Maggie's pulse jumped. She pulled her hand back too quickly.

Oliver just watched her. Not smirking. Not pushing. Just watching. Like he knew. Like he felt it too.

Maggie swallowed hard, gripping the counter. "This isn't normal."

Oliver tilted his head slightly. "No. It's not."

A beat. Then—

"So what are we gonna do about it?"

Chapter 16: Fighting the Inevitable

Maggie's brain shut down the second Oliver said it.

"So what are we gonna do about it?"

Because what kind of question was that? They weren't doing anything. This was just a weird week. An experiment. A fluke. Wasn't it?

Maggie gripped the edge of the counter like it might keep her steady. "We're not doing anything."

Oliver didn't move. Didn't blink. Didn't look convinced.

"Okay." His voice was slow, careful. "So you're telling me this is normal?"

Maggie scoffed. "We live together, Oliver. We just... exist in the same space."

His lips twitched, but not in amusement.

"Exist," he repeated.

Maggie nodded too quickly.

Oliver exhaled, rubbing the back of his neck. "So if I touch you right now—just for a second—you won't feel anything?"

Maggie's stomach flipped. He wasn't serious. Was he?

She narrowed her eyes. "You're being ridiculous."

Oliver took a step closer. Just one. Barely anything. But Maggie felt it everywhere.

Oliver's gaze never left hers.

"Go ahead," he said, voice even. "Say it again."

Maggie's throat went dry. "Say what?"

"That there's nothing here."

Her heart pounded. He was testing her. And worse? She was losing. Because even now—standing a few feet apart, barely touching— She felt him. Felt him like a ghost of every moment they'd ever had.

Every laugh. Every fight. Every kiss. Every single thing that made them them.

She clenched her jaw. "This is stupid."

Oliver nodded once. "You're right."

A long, unbearable pause.

Then—"So why do you look like you want me to prove you wrong?"

Maggie's pulse slammed into her ribs. She couldn't do this. Not right now. Not when her head was still too tangled in the past.

She turned sharply, grabbing the takeout container. "I'm eating in my office."

Oliver didn't stop her. Didn't call after her. Didn't push. But as she walked away, she heard it— A low chuckle. Soft. Almost fond. Like he already knew she wasn't going to win this fight.

Avoiding Oliver should have been easy. They lived under the same roof, but they had been living separately for months. Separate routines. Separate schedules. Separate everything.

But something was different now. Maggie could feel it. Even when he wasn't in the same room, she felt his presence in ways she hadn't before.

The coffee that was suddenly made before she got to the kitchen.The way he leaned against the counter, watching her just a second longer than necessary.

The way her body recognized every shift of his weight when he walked into a room. It was worse than fighting. Because at least with fighting—you knew where you stood. This? This was dangerous.

By the time Maggie finally emerged from her office, it was late. Too late. The house was dark except for the glow of the TV.

She hesitated in the doorway. Maybe he was asleep. But then— his voice cut through the quiet.

"You can stop avoiding me, you know."

Maggie flinched. "I'm not—"

Oliver turned his head from where he was stretched out on the couch, one arm slung lazily over the backrest.

He didn't even look annoyed. If anything, he looked...amused. Which somehow made it so much worse.

Maggie crossed her arms. "I'm not avoiding you."

Oliver just stared. That flat, unimpressed stare he always used to give her when she was lying.

Maggie huffed. "I'm not."

Oliver smirked, sipping his water. "Uh-huh."

A long pause.

Then, voice low—"Come sit, Hazard."

Maggie's stomach tightened. That nickname again. She should tell him to stop. Tell him it didn't mean anything. Tell him she wasn't playing this game.

Instead—she hesitated. And that hesitation ruined her. Because Oliver saw it. And Oliver knew exactly what it meant.

Maggie considered going upstairs. She should walk away. She should do anything other than what she was about to do. But her feet didn't listen.

Instead, before she could talk herself out of it, she crossed the room. Slow. Reluctant. Like someone stepping onto thin ice.

She perched on the farthest edge of the couch, body stiff. "Happy?"

Oliver watched her. "Getting there."

Maggie rolled her eyes. "You're impossible."

Oliver smirked. "And yet, here you are."

Maggie exhaled, shaking her head. But she didn't move. Because maybe—just maybe—she didn't want to.

Chapter 17: Softened Edges

Maggie didn't know why she stayed.

She could have gotten up after five minutes. Could have made some excuse, said she was tired, left the room before Oliver could make her feel anything more than she already did.

But she didn't. She stayed. Not close. Not comfortably. But there. And somehow, that was worse. Because the weight of everything unspoken between them sat right there in the space between them. And neither of them moved to fill it.

Oliver flipped through channels absentmindedly. He wasn't even watching, Maggie realized. Just filling the air with something other than silence.

Maggie curled her legs under herself, absently tucking her hands under her sweater sleeves.

They used to do this all the time. Just sit. Exist in the same space without expectation. And for a little while, it had been enough.

Maggie swallowed. "You're not even watching."

Oliver smirked but didn't look at her. "Neither are you."

Maggie rolled her eyes, but the corner of her mouth betrayed her.

And Oliver? He saw it. His smirk deepened just slightly, like he knew he was winning something he hadn't even been trying to win. And that? That irritated her.

Maggie shifted, stretching her legs out just slightly. "Remember when we used to do this?"

Oliver glanced at her. "Do what?"

"Sit like this. Not talking. Just... existing."

Oliver nodded slowly. "Yeah."

Maggie hummed. "I used to think that was one of the best things about us."

Oliver's brow lifted. "What?"

"That we didn't have to fill the space all the time."

Oliver exhaled, eyes flickering to the TV screen. "Yeah. Me too."

A pause.

Then—"So what happened?"

Maggie's stomach tightened. Because that was the real question, wasn't it? What happened? What went wrong?

Maggie let out a slow breath. "I don't know."

Oliver turned his head toward her. He didn't push. Didn't demand an answer. But he was waiting. Because he knew her. Knew that her I don't know wasn't the truth. Not really.

Maggie swallowed. "Maybe... Maybe we stopped seeing each other the way we used to."

Oliver didn't speak for a long time.

And when he finally did—his voice was quieter. "I never stopped seeing you."

Maggie's chest ached. Because he said it so simply. Like it wasn't a big revelation. Like it was just a fact. Something that had always been true. Something he had just been waiting for her to notice.

Maggie looked down at her hands, trying to ignore the way her stomach tightened. Because if she looked at him right now, she might do something reckless. And she wasn't ready for that. Not yet.

The room felt smaller. Maggie could hear the low hum of the TV, the soft rustle of fabric when Oliver shifted slightly beside her.

He didn't move closer. Didn't say anything else. He just let her sit with it. And maybe that was the problem.

Maybe Oliver never made demands. Maybe he just waited for her to figure it out on her own. And the worst part? Maggie didn't know if she could. The weight of everything between them sat heavy in the air. And Maggie? She needed an out.

She shifted, stretching her arms in an exaggerated motion. "I should go to bed."

Oliver nodded. "Yeah."

But he didn't move. Didn't make it easier for her. Didn't pull away first. And that was almost worse.

Maggie pushed herself up, forcing her legs to work. "Night, Oliver."

Oliver's gaze flickered to hers. And for a second—she thought he was going to say something. But he didn't. He just nodded once. And let her go.

Chapter 18: Memory Revived

Maggie hadn't slept well. She wasn't sure why she even bothered pulling the blankets over herself when she had spent most of the night staring at the ceiling, trying to push Oliver's words out of her head.

"I never stopped seeing you."

She hated him for that. Not because it wasn't true. But because she had spent so much time convincing herself that maybe it was. That maybe it was easier to believe they had both just... drifted.

Because if she let herself believe Oliver had always been there, waiting— That meant she was the one who left. And she didn't know how to sit with that.

Maggie came downstairs in desperate need of coffee. She had barely made it to the machine when Oliver walked in from outside. Hair damp. T-shirt sticking slightly to his back.

Maggie frowned. "You went running?"

Oliver pulled a water bottle from the fridge. "Yeah."

Maggie blinked. "You haven't done that in years."

Oliver smirked, unscrewing the cap. "Guess I do now."

Maggie rolled her eyes. Where had she heard that before? Still— it made her stomach twist. Because of course Oliver was doing something for himself. Something he used to love.

And Maggie was still standing in the same place. Still acting like she was stuck. Still avoiding every single thing that made her feel.

Maggie's day wasn't productive. She tried. She opened her laptop. Responded to some emails. Pretended to focus. But her mind wouldn't cooperate. She needed a break. Needed out of this house. Before she could talk herself out of it, she grabbed her keys and headed for the door.

"Going somewhere?" Oliver's voice was too casual.

Maggie sighed. "I just… need a drive."

Oliver studied her for a second. Then—he nodded. No questions. No pushing. Just let her go. And somehow, that made her chest ache even more.

Maggie didn't realize where she was driving until she pulled into the gravel lot. And the second she did—her stomach dropped. Because there, leaning against the railing at the edge of the lake, looking like he belonged there just as much as she did— Was Oliver.

Of course. Of course he was already here. Because this wasn't just her place. It was *theirs.* Always had been. And apparently— neither of them had ever really left.

Oliver turned at the sound of her footsteps. A flicker of surprise crossed his face—but not much. Like some part of him expected her to show up.

Maggie crossed her arms. "You still come here?"

Oliver nodded. "Always have."

Maggie swallowed. So had she. She just... never thought to look for him.

She turned toward the water, eyes locked on the steady ripples against the dock. "I thought I was the only one."

Oliver exhaled. "Guess not."

Silence. Not heavy. Not suffocating. Just full. Full of everything they had forgotten. Everything they had let slip away.

Maggie stepped forward, toeing the edge of the dock. She could feel Oliver watching her. Like he knew exactly what she was thinking. Because they had been here before. Years ago. A summer night. A dare.

"I'll jump if you jump."

They had been young. Reckless. Happy. And Oliver had kept his word. He always did. He had jumped. She had followed. And they had laughed until they couldn't breathe. Dripping. Shivering. Holding onto each other like it was the only thing that mattered.

Maggie swallowed hard. Because suddenly—she wasn't sure if she had ever felt that free again. Not since that night. Not since before things got hard. Not since she stopped reaching for him the way she used to.

Maggie turned her head slightly. "Do you ever miss it?"

Oliver didn't ask what. Because he knew.

His voice was quiet. "Every day."

Maggie's stomach twisted. Because that was the thing about Oliver. He never made things complicated. Never danced around emotions the way she did. He just... felt. And now?

Now Maggie couldn't pretend not to see it anymore. Couldn't pretend she wasn't feeling it too.

Oliver shifted beside her, close enough that she could feel the warmth of him. But he didn't move closer. Didn't touch her. Didn't push. Just let her sit in it. Let her feel whatever this was.

And Maggie felt everything. For the first time in a long time—she didn't run from it. She just stood there. Next to him.

Looking out at the place that still held all their best memories. And wondering—just maybe—if there were still more to come.

Chapter 19: The First Step

Maggie wasn't sure what changed. Maybe it was the way Oliver had looked at her at the lake.

Maybe it was the memory of him saying, "I never stopped seeing you."

Maybe it was the realization that she was the one who had stopped looking. Either way—something shifted. Because for the first time in a long time, Maggie wasn't just thinking about what they had lost. She was thinking about what was still there. And for the first time—she wanted to reach for it.

Maggie walked into the kitchen the next morning, her heart pounding harder than it should. Oliver was already there. Sitting at the table, scrolling through his phone, looking completely at ease.

Like he belonged there. Which, of course, he did. But Maggie had spent so long pretending not to see him. Now, she felt every inch of space between them. And for the first time—she wanted to close it.

She cleared her throat. "Coffee?"

Oliver blinked, looking up. "Huh?"

Maggie lifted the mug in her hand. It was stupid, really. Something so small. But they hadn't made coffee for each other in... she couldn't even remember how long.

Oliver's brows lifted slightly, like he wasn't sure what to make of it. But after a beat—he nodded.

"Yeah. Thanks."

Maggie poured him a cup. No big deal. Just coffee. Just a habit they had long since abandoned. But when she set it in front of him, Oliver's fingers brushed hers. And the shock of warmth that traveled through her was anything but small.

Oliver felt it too. She knew he did. Because when she looked up, he was already watching her. Not like this was just coffee. Not like this was nothing. But like he knew exactly what it was.

A first step. A quiet, unspoken choice. One Maggie had made all on her own.

They sat at the table together. Not awkward. Not quite normal, either. Something in between. Maggie took a sip of her coffee, trying to ignore the way Oliver's presence felt different now. Or maybe—she was the one who was different. She was the one letting herself feel it.

The quiet. The weight of the past. The possibilities of the future.It was terrifying. But for once—she didn't want to run from it.

Oliver set his cup down, his gaze steady. "So what happens now?"

Maggie's stomach twisted. Because that was the question, wasn't it? Where did they go from here?

Maggie inhaled slowly. "I don't know."

And for once, she wasn't avoiding the truth. Oliver nodded, as if he expected that answer. But instead of pressing—he just took another sip of his coffee.

Like he was willing to wait. Like he had always been willing to wait. And for the first time in a long time—Maggie didn't hate the idea of figuring it out.

Chapter 20: The Second Step

Maggie wasn't naive. She knew that one cup of coffee didn't erase everything that had happened between them. Didn't magically fix their distance. Didn't rewrite the years of missed moments and unspoken words. But it was a start. And that was something.

The next day, Maggie stood at the bottom of the staircase, debating. Oliver was upstairs, working in his office. She could hear the faint sound of him moving papers around, typing occasionally. He was busy.

Maggie took a breath, walked up, and knocked lightly on the open door.

Oliver looked up, eyebrows lifting slightly in surprise. "Hey."

Maggie shifted, suddenly regretting this. "Hey."

Oliver leaned back in his chair. "What's up?"

Maggie hesitated. This was stupid. She should just say never mind. But instead—

"I was going to make dinner."

Oliver blinked. And for a second, he didn't say anything.

Then—his mouth twitched. "You cook now?"

Maggie scowled. "I cook fine."

Oliver chuckled, the sound too easy. Too familiar. "Sure."

Maggie huffed, crossing her arms. "Forget it."

She turned, ready to walk away— But then Oliver's voice stopped her.

"Hey, Mags."

She paused. Oliver's voice was softer now.

"You making enough for two?"

Maggie's stomach tightened. Because he knew what she was really asking. Knew that this wasn't about food. It was about sitting down together. It was about trying.

She swallowed. "Yeah."

Oliver exhaled slowly. "Then I'm in."

Cooking wasn't Maggie's strong suit. Oliver knew it. She knew Oliver knew it. But he didn't comment. Didn't tease her when she had to double-check the seasoning or when she got distracted and almost burned the bread.

He just leaned against the counter, sipping a beer, watching her. Not in a way that made her self-conscious. Just watching.

Like he was trying to figure her out all over again. Like she was someone worth paying attention to. Maggie's stomach twisted. Because when was the last time she had felt that? The weight of someone's focus. The quiet warmth of being seen.

She cleared her throat, turning back to the stove. She needed to focus.

They sat across from each other at the table. Maggie's knee bounced slightly under the table, like her body didn't quite know what to do with itself.

Oliver didn't say much at first. Just ate. And for a second, Maggie thought this might be normal. Until—

"This is good," Oliver said, swallowing a bite.

Maggie blinked. "You sound surprised."

Oliver smirked. "A little."

Maggie scoffed, tossing a piece of bread at him. Oliver caught it, grinning. And suddenly—the air shifted.

Because that was them. The teasing. The easy banter. It had always been the best part. And Maggie had missed it. More than she wanted to admit.

They cleaned up together. Not in a way that felt forced. Just... natural. Oliver rinsed the dishes, Maggie dried. Like muscle memory.

And when she handed him the last plate, Oliver took it—but didn't move away. For just a second too long, they stood too close. The kitchen suddenly felt too small.

Maggie's breath caught. Because Oliver wasn't moving. And worse? Neither was she.

Oliver's fingers were still wrapped around the plate, but his eyes— His eyes were on her. Steady. Familiar. Like he could see right through her.

Maggie's pulse pounded. Because this wasn't nothing. This wasn't just nostalgia. This was something else. Something too big. Something too dangerous.

And Maggie panicked. She took a step back, breaking the moment.

"I'm gonna head up."

Oliver didn't argue. Didn't stop her. But before she could leave, he called out—

"Hey, Mags."

She hesitated. Oliver smirked. Just slightly.

"Dinner was good."

Maggie's throat tightened. Because that wasn't about dinner at all. It was about this. About them.

And Maggie didn't know what to do with that yet.

So she just nodded. "Goodnight, Oliver."

Then walked away. Even though some small part of her wanted to stay.

Chapter 21: The Question She Can't Ignore

Maggie had always been good at avoidance. It was a skill. A survival tactic.

And when she woke up the morning after dinner with Oliver, she tried to lean on it. Tried to pretend like she hadn't almost let something happen in the kitchen. Tried to act like she hadn't spent half the night staring at the ceiling, wondering what would've happened if she hadn't stepped back.

But the problem with trying to forget something like that? It only made it louder.

Oliver wasn't in the kitchen when Maggie came down. His shoes were by the door, keys missing from the hook—he had gone out.

For a second, Maggie felt relief. Because space was good. Space meant she had time to breathe. But then—she saw it. A mug on the counter.

Not just any mug. Her mug. And next to it? A second one. Fresh coffee. Waiting for her. Maggie's breath caught. Because this wasn't just habit. This was intentional.

This was Oliver saying I thought about you before I left. And Maggie wasn't ready for what that meant.

Maggie was still staring at the coffee when Gina called. She almost didn't answer. But then—she needed the distraction. So she swiped the screen.

"Hey."

Gina's voice was too smug. "How's the experiment going?"

Maggie groaned, pinching the bridge of her nose. "Please don't call it that."

Gina laughed. "Okay, fine. How's coexisting going?"

Maggie hesitated. Because what was she supposed to say? That Oliver was different. That she was different. That somehow—this week wasn't going the way she expected at all. So instead, she went with—

"It's fine."

Gina wasn't buying it. "Fine?"

"Yes, Gina. Fine."

A pause.

Then—"Do you want it to be fine?"

Maggie's stomach twisted. Because that was the real question, wasn't it? Did she want this—whatever it was—to just be fine? Did she want to walk away from this week with nothing changed? Or did she want more?

Maggie swallowed. "I don't know."

Gina hummed. "That's not a no."

Maggie closed her eyes, sighing. "I know."

Oliver got back in the early afternoon. Maggie was in the living room, curled up with her laptop, trying to work but failing miserably.

She glanced up when the door shut. Oliver kicked off his shoes, running a hand through his hair.

"Where'd you go?" Maggie asked, before she could stop herself.

Oliver tossed his keys onto the counter. "Nowhere important."

Maggie hesitated. "You, uh... you left coffee."

Oliver leaned against the counter, crossing his arms. "Yeah."

Maggie frowned. That's it?

She exhaled. "Why?"

Oliver's eyes flickered toward hers. "Do I need a reason?"

Maggie opened her mouth—then closed it. Because she didn't have an answer. Not one she liked. Because this was different. Because it meant something.

And Maggie was finally starting to admit to herself that she might want it to.

Chapter 22: The Moment She Stops Running

Maggie hadn't stopped thinking about it. The coffee. The conversation with Gina. The way Oliver didn't press, didn't push—but still managed to get under her skin anyway. She wanted to ignore it. Wanted to pretend nothing had changed. But the truth was? Everything had.

That night, Maggie stood in front of the bathroom mirror, hands braced on the sink, staring at herself. Her reflection didn't give her any answers. Didn't tell her why her chest felt tight every time Oliver looked at her like he was waiting for her to figure something out. Didn't explain why she had spent so long convincing herself she didn't care—only to realize that maybe she still did.

But avoiding it wasn't working. Pretending wasn't working. And for once, Maggie was tired of running. She exhaled. Then, before she could talk herself out of it, she made her way downstairs.

Oliver was in the kitchen, leaning against the counter, flipping through a book. He looked up when she walked in. "Couldn't sleep?"

Maggie hesitated. Then—she shook her head.

"No, I—" She cleared her throat. This was harder than she thought. "I was thinking about going for a drive."

Oliver's brows lifted slightly. "Yeah?"

Maggie nodded. Here was the real test.

"You wanna come?"

A pause. Something unreadable flickered in Oliver's gaze. Like he knew this meant something. Like he wasn't sure if she did. Then— he nodded.

"Yeah," he said quietly. "Yeah, I do."

Maggie didn't know where they were going. She just drove. Windows cracked, night air slipping in. The radio played low— some old song neither of them acknowledged but both of them knew.

And for a long time—they didn't speak. Not because there was nothing to say. But because for the first time in a long time, the silence didn't feel heavy. It just... was. Like the way it used to be. Like a part of them had never left.

Maggie didn't realize where she had driven until she pulled into the overlook. The place they used to go when they just needed to breathe.

She let out a quiet, almost amused exhale. Of course.

Oliver smirked. "Didn't think you even remembered this place."

Maggie shot him a look. "I could say the same about you."

Oliver just chuckled, shaking his head. And when Maggie finally turned off the engine—neither of them moved.

Maggie's fingers drummed against the steering wheel. Then, before she could stop herself—

"Why didn't we do this before?"

Oliver exhaled. "Do what?"

Maggie swallowed. Why was this so hard?

"Talk," she said quietly.

Oliver was quiet for a long time. Then—he spoke.

"You didn't want to."

Maggie's breath hitched. Because he wasn't wrong. Not really. She had spent so long avoiding, shutting down, pulling away.

Oliver had let her. Because what was he supposed to do? Force her to care?

Maggie's fingers curled in her lap.

"I think I just got... lost," she admitted.

It wasn't an excuse. Just a truth.

Oliver nodded slowly. "I know."

Maggie turned her head, studying him. "Do you?"

Oliver's gaze met hers. "Yeah," he said, voice steady. "I do."

And Maggie? Maggie believed him. For the first time in a long time, she believed him.

Oliver turned back toward the windshield, tapping his fingers against his knee. And Maggie—she couldn't stop looking at him.

At the way his jaw tensed slightly, like there were a hundred things he wanted to say but wasn't sure if he should.

At the way he still fit so perfectly in the passenger seat beside her. At the way she was suddenly hit with the overwhelming urge to reach for him. Her hand twitched on the console.

Oliver noticed. She knew he did—because his eyes flickered toward her just slightly. Like he was waiting. Like he was giving her the choice.

Maggie swallowed. Then—she chickened out. She cleared her throat, shifting in her seat.

"We should probably head back."

Oliver nodded once, expression unreadable.

"Yeah," he said, voice even. "Probably."

But neither of them moved. Not yet. Because the moment wasn't over. Not really. It had just been postponed.

For the first time—Maggie wasn't sure if she wanted to keep delaying it.

Chapter 23: The Realization She Can't Ignore

Maggie spent the next day pretending nothing had happened. Pretending she hadn't driven Oliver to their old spot. Pretending she hadn't almost reached for him. Pretending she hadn't felt something shift inside her. But the thing about pretending? It never lasts.

Oliver was already in the kitchen when Maggie came down that morning. He was at the stove, cooking. That was new.

Maggie hesitated in the doorway. "Since when do you make breakfast?"

Oliver glanced over his shoulder. "Since I needed a distraction."

Maggie swallowed. That was familiar. That was what he had said at the restaurant. When she had first realized he had been teaching himself to cook.

Maggie crossed her arms, leaning against the counter. "You okay?"

Oliver didn't answer right away. Instead, he flipped a pancake onto a plate, then turned toward her.

"Are you?"

Maggie's breath hitched. Because that wasn't the question she had expected. And worse? She didn't have an answer. Maggie inhaled slowly, gripping the edge of the counter.

"I don't know," she admitted.

Oliver nodded once, like he understood. Like he had expected that answer. Then—he slid a plate in front of her.

Maggie frowned. "What's this?"

Oliver smirked. "Breakfast."

Maggie raised a brow. "You made this for me?"

Oliver shrugged. "Guess I did."

Maggie's stomach twisted. Because this was different. This wasn't habit. This was effort.

And Maggie wasn't sure what to do with it. She picked up her fork, but she didn't eat right away. She just... stared at the plate. And suddenly—she wasn't here.

She was somewhere else. Years ago. A different morning. A younger version of Oliver standing in front of the stove, fumbling with a spatula.

"Babe, I'm serious. You're gonna eat this and pretend it's the best thing you've ever had."

Maggie had laughed. Had stolen the spatula from his hand. Had kissed him on the cheek before taking over.

She had forgotten about that morning. Had forgotten about so many mornings like it. But sitting here now, with Oliver watching her—it all came rushing back.

Maggie picked up her fork. Took a bite. Swallowed past the lump in her throat. Then—she looked at Oliver. And for the first time in a long time—she let herself see him.

Not just as the person she had been coexisting with. But as the man she had once loved so deeply she couldn't imagine a world without him. And maybe, just maybe— She wasn't ready to lose that yet.

Chapter 24: The First Real Step

Maggie had spent so much time waiting. Waiting for something to change. Waiting for time to fix things. Waiting for the right moment.

But maybe that had been the problem all along. Because waiting never fixed anything. Not in life. Not in love. And definitely not with Oliver. So for once—she wasn't going to wait. She was going to do something about it.

Maggie waited until Oliver had finished cleaning up the kitchen. Waited until she was sure she wasn't going to back out. Then— before she could overthink it, she spoke.

"You wanna get out of here for a bit?"

Oliver turned, brows lifting slightly. "What?"

Maggie swallowed. "I was thinking about going for a walk. Thought maybe you'd wanna come."

Oliver studied her. Not suspicious. Just... curious. Like he knew this meant something. And he was waiting to see if she did, too. Then—he nodded.

"Yeah," he said simply. "Let's go."

The air was warm but breezy. The sun had started to dip lower in the sky, casting everything in a soft, golden glow. It should have felt normal.

But it didn't. Not with Oliver walking beside her. Not with the way their arms kept brushing. Not with the way Maggie was suddenly hyper-aware of every inch of space between them. Or rather—how little space there was.

They walked in silence for a while. Not tense. Not uncomfortable. Just full. Full of everything unspoken. Then—Oliver spoke first.

"Why now?"

Maggie's breath caught. She knew what he was asking. Not about the walk. Not about tonight. But about her. About why she was finally letting herself be here with him. Maggie exhaled slowly, watching her feet move over the pavement.

"I don't know."

Oliver hummed. "Yeah, you do."

Maggie's stomach twisted. Because he wasn't wrong. She did know. She had just been too scared to say it. But wasn't that the whole point of this? She wasn't waiting anymore. She was *choosing*. So, finally—she admitted it.

"I miss you," she said softly.

She didn't look at him. Couldn't. Not when she had just said the one thing she had been trying to ignore for months.

Oliver was silent. And for a second, Maggie thought she had ruined everything. But then—he stopped walking. And when Maggie finally forced herself to look up at him—

Oliver was already watching her. Watching her like she had just said the most important thing in the world.

Oliver exhaled, running a hand through his hair.

"Mags..."

His voice was rough. Like he didn't trust himself to speak.

Maggie's heart pounded.

Because this was it. This was the part where she either leaned in—or ran. She had run before. She wasn't going to do it again. So, before she could talk herself out of it—she took a step closer.

Small. Hesitant. But toward him.

And Oliver noticed. His breath hitched. His hands flexed at his sides. Like he wanted to reach for her—but was waiting for her to do it first.

Maggie swallowed hard. Then, voice barely above a whisper—

"I don't want to do this without you."

Oliver closed his eyes for half a second. Like he had been waiting to hear that for longer than she realized. Then—he nodded.

"Okay."

Maggie blinked. "Okay?"

Oliver looked at her. And she took a deep breath. She had forgotten how intense his eyes could be.

"Okay," he repeated, softer this time. "Then let's figure it out."

Maggie exhaled.

And for the first time in a long time—she wasn't scared. Because this wasn't a maybe. This wasn't a question. This was a choice.

And Maggie was finally ready to make it.

Chapter 25: The Test That Changes Everything

Maggie hadn't realized how easy it was to say the words. I miss you. I don't want to do this without you. But now, standing in the quiet of their home, she realized—saying it was the easy part.

The hard part? Following through. Because this wasn't just a conversation. This was them. This was deciding whether they were willing to put in the work.

And Maggie had never been more terrified.

That night, everything felt different. The way Oliver moved around the house. The way Maggie found herself watching him. The way the air between them felt charged in a way it hadn't in a long time.

She wasn't avoiding him anymore.

And Oliver was still waiting. Still letting her set the pace. And somehow—that was worse. Because it meant this was real. It meant he was letting her make the choice. And Maggie? She didn't want to run anymore.

It started with a storm. The kind that crept in without warning, thunder rolling low in the distance as the wind shifted suddenly. Maggie had just stepped outside to bring in the mail when the first drops hit.

By the time she reached the porch—it was pouring. And of course—Oliver had just pulled into the driveway. Maggie turned, squinting through the rain as Oliver stepped out of the car.

Their eyes met. And for some reason—they both just... stood there. Like they were waiting to see who would move first.

The rain was cold, heavy. And yet—neither of them moved. Until Oliver suddenly laughed. Shook his head, wiped the water from his face. And Maggie laughed too. Because what else were they supposed to do?

Oliver jogged up the porch steps, rain dripping from his hair. Maggie stepped back to give him space, but Oliver didn't step inside right away. Instead, he looked at her. Really looked at her.

And suddenly—Maggie wasn't thinking about the rain. She was thinking about how close they were standing. How easy it would be for him to reach for her. How easy it would be for her to let him.

Oliver exhaled. "This feels familiar."

Maggie swallowed. "Yeah."

Because it did. It felt like them. Like before. Like all the nights they had spent running through summer storms. Like all the moments when they had been young and reckless and madly in love. And Maggie had missed it. More than she had ever let herself admit.

Oliver's gaze dropped—just for a second. Maggie felt it everywhere. The way his eyes flickered to her lips. The way he swayed just slightly toward her. The way the space between them suddenly felt too small.

Her heart slammed against her ribs. And for a second—she thought he was going to kiss her. She wanted him to. She *really* wanted him to. But instead—Oliver just studied her. Then, softly—

"Tell me what you want, Maggie."

Maggie's breath hitched.

Because that was it, wasn't it? He wasn't going to push. He wasn't going to take the choice away from her. This was on her. And suddenly—she knew. She knew exactly what she wanted. She wanted this. She wanted him.

But before she could say it—the porch light flickered. The power cut out. And just like that—the moment was gone. The house was dark when they stepped inside. Maggie exhaled, wiping the rain from her arms.

"Well. That was dramatic."

Oliver smirked. "Fitting."

A beat of silence. Then—Maggie turned to face him. And even in the dark—she could feel him watching her. She didn't move. Didn't look away. Didn't run.

Instead—she made a decision. Softly, hesitantly—she reached for his hand. And Oliver let her. Because maybe—finally—Maggie was done waiting.

Chapter 26: The Moment She Finally Wants

Maggie didn't let go of Oliver's hand. Not when they stood there, rain dripping from their clothes. Not when the house sat in darkness around them. Not when Oliver's fingers tightened around hers.

Because for the first time in a long time—she wasn't afraid of touching him. She wasn't afraid of what it meant. She was afraid of how much she wanted it. But for once—she wasn't running from that. Not anymore.

Oliver broke the silence first. His voice was quiet. Careful. Like he wasn't sure if he should say it.

"This feels familiar."

Maggie swallowed. Because he wasn't wrong. It did. The darkened house. The storm outside. The way they were standing close but not quite touching. It felt like the nights they used to steal before life got too loud. Before responsibility. Before stress. Before everything became something they had to fight for.

Maggie inhaled. "Yeah."

Oliver's thumb brushed absently against her palm. And suddenly—the memory was sharp. Years ago. A power outage. A thunderstorm. Huddling close, laughing in the dark.

"If I can't see you, does that mean you're not real?"

Maggie had smiled.

Had taken his hands, pulled him close.

"I'm real."

She had kissed him first that night. Had wanted him first. And now? She was so very tired of being afraid of wanting him.

Maggie didn't let herself overthink it. Didn't let herself talk herself out of it. She stepped closer—just slightly. Enough that Oliver noticed. Enough that he exhaled carefully.

"Mags."

She loved the way he said her name. Like it still meant something. Like she still meant something. And maybe—she did. Maybe she always had. So she whispered—

"I'm real."

And *finally*—she kissed him.

It wasn't slow. Wasn't tentative. Because there was no hesitation left. Because this wasn't just a kiss. This was a choice. A breaking of everything that had been holding her back.

Oliver's hands found her waist, pulling her closer. Maggie let him. Let herself fall into him. Because she wanted this. And for once—she wasn't afraid to show it.

Oliver pulled back just enough to look at her. His breathing was uneven. His grip steady but not demanding. Like he was giving her the chance to stop. Like he was still waiting for her to be sure.

Maggie exhaled. And she was. She had never been so sure. She brushed her fingers along the edge of his jaw. Soft. Deliberate. And then, voice barely above a whisper—

"Come upstairs with me."

Oliver didn't hesitate. Didn't ask if she was sure. Because he could see it. For the first time—Maggie wasn't running. She was reaching for him.

And Oliver was done waiting.

Chapter 27: The Night That Changes Everything

Maggie led Oliver upstairs. Her pulse hammered. Not with doubt. Not with hesitation. But with certainty. Because for the first time in years, she wasn't scared of wanting this. Of wanting him. Of choosing him.

And Oliver? He let her lead. Because this was her choice. And he wasn't going to take that away from her.

They reached the bedroom, and Maggie turned. Oliver was watching her. Not with expectation. Not with assumption. But with patience. Like he was still giving her the space to change her mind. To step back. To run.

But Maggie was done running. So, before she could overthink it— she reached for him. Her fingers curled around the front of his shirt, and Oliver inhaled sharply—like he hadn't been sure she'd do it.

And Maggie needed him to be sure. So she whispered, "Stay."

Oliver lifted a hand, fingers tracing along her jaw—gentle, but grounding. Like he was memorizing her. Like he needed to be sure she was real. Maggie leaned into it, eyes fluttering closed for just a second. Because she had missed this. She hadn't even realized how much.

Oliver's voice was barely above a whisper.

"You sure?"

Maggie exhaled, meeting his gaze. No fear. No doubt. Just this.

"Yeah," she breathed. "I'm sure."

And Oliver kissed her like he believed her. It wasn't rushed. It wasn't desperate. It was intentional. A rediscovery. A remembering.

Maggie traced her hands over the planes of his back, feeling every inch of him that she had once known by heart.

And Oliver mapped her skin like he was piecing together something he had never really lost. And in that moment—Maggie realized something.

She hadn't stopped wanting him. She had just forgotten how to let herself have him. But she wasn't holding back. Not anymore.

Afterward, in the tranquil aftermath Maggie lay against Oliver's chest, his arm wrapped loosely around her. The room was dark. Quiet. But not empty.

Maggie traced absent patterns against his skin. Felt the steady rise and fall of his breath.

And for the first time *in a long time*—she felt at peace. Oliver shifted slightly, pressing a kiss to the top of her head. Soft. Thoughtless. Natural. Like he had never forgotten how to hold her.

Maggie swallowed hard. Because this wasn't just a moment. It was a choice. And for the first time—she wasn't afraid of what came next.

Chapter 28: The Morning After Everything Changed

Maggie woke to the feeling of warmth. Solid. Steady. Familiar. For a second—she didn't move. Didn't open her eyes. Didn't acknowledge the shift in the air. Because the second she did—this would be real.

The night before. The way she had reached for Oliver. The way he had held her like she was still his. And maybe—*just maybe*—she was.

She blinked her eyes open slowly. The early morning light filtered softly through the curtains. And next to her—Oliver was already awake. Watching her.

Maggie's stomach twisted. Not in fear. Not in regret. But in knowing. Because they had crossed a line. Not a reckless, impulsive line. Not a mistake. But a choice. And now—they had to figure out what it meant.

Oliver's voice was rough with sleep.

"Morning."

Maggie swallowed. "Morning."

Silence. Not heavy. Not awkward. Just... full.

Oliver shifted slightly, head propped against his arm as he studied her.

Then, softly—"You okay?"

Maggie's heart stumbled. Because he wasn't asking if last night was a mistake. He wasn't questioning what they had done. He was checking on *her*.

And Maggie? She was okay. For the first time in a long time—she was okay.

So she nodded. "Yeah."

Oliver exhaled, relieved. And then—he smiled. Small. Just a flicker. But it made Maggie's chest ache. Because she had seriously missed that.

Maggie sat up slowly, pulling the sheet with her. She needed a second. Needed to breathe. But the second she moved—Oliver sat up too. Not to stop her. Just to be with her.

"Mags."

His voice was gentle. Like he could feel her bracing for something. Like he wasn't sure if she was about to run.

And Maggie almost did. Because old habits don't just disappear overnight. But instead—she closed her eyes. Took a slow breath. And chose to stay.

When she looked at him again, Oliver was still watching her. Still waiting. Like he always had. And Maggie was so tired of making him wait. So, instead of pulling away—she spoke.

"I don't know what happens next."

Oliver exhaled.

Then, softly—

"Me neither."

Maggie let out a breath she didn't realize she had been holding. Because this wasn't a demand. This wasn't pressure. This was figuring it out together. And for the first time—that didn't scare her.

Maggie glanced toward the door.

"I should probably make coffee."

Oliver smirked, shifting closer. "Or—"

Maggie raised a brow. "Or?"

Oliver leaned in slightly, not quite touching. But close enough that she could feel him.

"Or we could stay here for a little while longer."

Maggie's pulse jumped. Not because she was scared. But because she wasn't. Because she wanted that. She wanted him. And finally—she let herself have it.

So instead of answering—she kissed him.

And Oliver kissed her back. Because this wasn't hesitation anymore. This was a beginning.

And Maggie was finally ready to take it.

Chapter 29: The Space Between Then and Now

The morning stretched on in quiet contentment. They didn't rush. Didn't leap to define what last night meant. And maybe that was what made it different.

For the first time in a long time— Maggie wasn't rushing to figure things out. She was just letting herself be here. Letting herself want Oliver and he was letting her.

Maggie made it to the kitchen—eventually. Oliver followed a few minutes later, hair still mussed, shirt hanging loose.

And darn—that did something to her. Because this was different. Different from all the mornings where they had moved around each other like ghosts.

Now, when Oliver walked in—she felt it. Now, when he reached for a mug—her breath caught. Because she wasn't just noticing him. She was allowing herself to feel it.

Oliver leaned against the counter, watching her.

Maggie raised an eyebrow. "What?"

Oliver smirked. "You tell me."

Maggie rolled her eyes, but she was smiling. Because it was easy. Because it was them.

Oliver exhaled, shifting slightly. "So—what now?"

Maggie's stomach should have twisted. Should have clenched with nerves. But instead—she felt calm. Because she already knew her answer.

So she took a sip of her coffee, met his gaze, and simply said—"We see where this goes."

Oliver blinked. Not because he was surprised. But because maybe he hadn't expected it to be that simple.

And maybe—neither had she. But it was. It really was. Because they had already spent so long making things difficult.

And Maggie was done with that.

Later that afternoon, Maggie got a text from Gina.

Gina: Drinks. Tonight. No excuses.

Maggie huffed a small laugh.

Because of course.

Gina wasn't the type to let things sit quietly.

Maggie hesitated for only a second before typing back—

Maggie: Fine. But you're paying for the first round.

Gina: Fair. Bring Oliver.

Maggie's breath hitched.

Because Gina knew.

Of course she knew.

Maggie hesitated.

Then, before she could overthink it, she turned to Oliver.

"Wanna go out tonight?"

Oliver raised a brow. "With?"

"Gina."

Oliver smirked. "And Jake?"

Maggie groaned. "Probably."

Oliver leaned against the couch. "Is this a test?"

Maggie narrowed her eyes. "Of what?"

"Of... us."

Maggie exhaled. "No. It's just drinks."

Oliver watched her for a long moment.

Then—he nodded.

"Alright, Mags. Let's do it."

And Maggie?

She was oddly excited to see what would happen next.

Chapter 30: The First Step Into the Real World

Maggie had been fine—right up until they arrived at the bar. Then, suddenly—she wasn't. Because this was different. This wasn't just them, alone in their house, figuring things out in quiet moments.

This was public. This was Gina and Jake. This was other people seeing them together—and noticing. And Maggie wasn't sure what that would look like.

Oliver parked, glanced over at her.

"You okay?"

Maggie exhaled, gripping the edge of her seat. "Yeah."

Oliver just looked at her. Like he knew she was full of it. Maggie groaned, leaning her head back against the seat.

"Okay, fine. I don't know."

Oliver smirked. "I figured."

Maggie narrowed her eyes. "Is this funny to you?"

Oliver shrugged. "A little."

Maggie sighed. "You're enjoying this way too much."

Oliver leaned in slightly, voice low, teasing.

"Maybe."

Maggie's stomach flipped.

She rolled her eyes, shoving the door open. "Let's get this over with."

Oliver chuckled. "That's the spirit."

The second they walked in—Gina saw them. Her brows shot up, and then she nudged Jake hard. Jake turned, saw them, and immediately smirked.

Great. This was going to be a thing. Maggie braced herself as they approached the table.

Gina grinned. "Well, well, well."

Maggie sighed. "Don't."

Gina ignored her, eyes flicking between them. "So. This is happening."

Maggie grabbed a menu, pretended to be intensely interested in it. Oliver, on the other hand? He was completely unfazed.

He slid into a seat, stretching his arm along the back of Maggie's chair.

Jake smirked. "So, you two finally figured it out?"

Oliver shrugged. "Something like that."

Maggie groaned. "I hate all of you."

Jake grinned. "You love us."

Gina nodded. "She does."

Maggie sighed. This was a mistake.

The teasing settled down—eventually. But the knowing looks didn't. Gina tapped her fingers against her glass, watching Maggie carefully.

Then—"So, what's different this time?"

Maggie blinked. "What?"

Gina shrugged. "You and Oliver. What makes this different?"

Maggie hesitated. Because that was a fair question. A hard one. She thought about the past few days. The small moments. The quiet changes. The way she had stopped waiting and started choosing. And finally—she had her answer.

Maggie glanced at Oliver. He was already looking at her. Like he knew exactly what she was thinking. And so—she told Gina the truth.

"I stopped being scared of wanting it."

Gina blinked. Jake raised a brow. Oliver just smiled. And Maggie felt lighter. Because for the first time in *a long time*—she had stopped running. And maybe that was all the difference in the world.

Chapter 31: The Quiet, Steady Choice

Maggie hadn't expected relief. But that's what this was. Sitting across from Gina and Jake, Oliver's arm draped casually along the back of her chair.

It wasn't some big announcement. It wasn't some grand proclamation. It was just... them. No more hiding. No more pretending.

And Maggie hadn't realized how much she had been waiting to exhale.

After the teasing died down, conversation shifted. Talk of work, Gina's latest obsession with paddleboarding, Jake's fantasy football disaster.

Normal things. Things that had nothing to do with Maggie and Oliver. And for the first time—Maggie let herself settle. Because it wasn't them against the world. It wasn't them being analyzed. It was just a night out with people who cared about them. And maybe—that mattered more than she realized.

They said their goodbyes in the parking lot. Gina grinned too knowingly as she hugged Maggie. Jake clapped Oliver on the back like he had won some kind of prize. And when they got to the car—Oliver hesitated.

Maggie raised a brow. "What?"

Oliver exhaled, leaning against the passenger door.

"I liked that."

Maggie blinked. "Liked what?"

Oliver looked at her, expression softer than she expected.

"Not having to pretend."

Maggie's breath hitched. Because yeah. That was it, wasn't it? This time, they weren't trying to force anything. They weren't trying to prove anything. They were just... being. And somehow—that made all the difference.

The drive home was quiet. Not awkward. Not heavy. Just... comfortable. Maggie let herself steal a glance at Oliver.

The way his fingers tapped absently against the wheel. The way he seemed at ease. Not waiting for the other shoe to drop. Not waiting for Maggie to change her mind. Because maybe—he finally believed she wouldn't. And maybe—that mattered more than anything else.

When they got home, Maggie kicked off her shoes, stretching. Oliver watched her, leaning against the counter.

Maggie narrowed her eyes. "What?"

Oliver smirked. "You good?"

Maggie rolled her eyes. "You always ask that."

Oliver shrugged. "Because I always mean it."

Maggie hesitated. Then—she closed the space between them. Not a lot. Just enough. And then—she reached for his hand. Oliver's breath caught. Maggie squeezed lightly, a quiet confirmation.

"I'm good."

Oliver exhaled. And maybe—that was all he needed to hear.

Chapter 32: The Unexpected Vulnerability

Maggie had thought she was done being nervous. Thought she had crossed the hard part. But the next morning, reality settled in. Because last night was easy. Last night was familiar. Last night was Oliver, teasing her in the car, watching her across the table, brushing his hand against hers like it wasn't a big deal.

And maybe—that was what scared her the most. Because it was easy to fall into this. But what happened when it wasn't easy anymore?

She found Oliver in the kitchen. Again.

Maggie blinked. "Are you officially the breakfast guy now?"

Oliver grinned. "Maybe."

Maggie crossed her arms, watching him move. There was something about it. The way he stood comfortably in their space. The way he didn't overthink it. The way he hadn't tried to talk about last night—just let it be.

And Maggie? She appreciated that. Because she wasn't ready to define it. Not yet. But she wasn't scared of it, either. So, instead of overthinking—she sat down. And for the first time in a long time—she let herself just enjoy the morning.

Later that afternoon, Maggie was going through some old things. Just Organizing. Trying to get rid of some of the clutter she had ignored for too long.

She hadn't meant to dig up the past. But there it was—a small, dust-covered box, tucked away in the back of the closet. And the second she opened it—the years melted away.

Tiny shoes. A hospital bracelet. A sonogram photo. Her breath hitched. Because she had forgotten it was here. Had forgotten that she had saved these things. And yet—she hadn't let them go. She never could.

Maggie didn't hear Oliver come in. Didn't notice him at all—not until his voice broke through the silence.

"Maggie?"

She flinched. Her hands clenched around the tiny shoe in her palm.

Oliver's voice softened instantly. "Mags?"

And when she finally lifted her gaze—he saw. Saw the box. Saw what was inside. Saw what she wasn't saying.

His face changed. Like someone had knocked the air out of him. But instead of speaking—he moved. He dropped down beside her on the floor, his body warm and solid and right there. And then— he pulled her into his arms.

Maggie let him. Because there was no fighting it. No pretending this didn't still sit between them. Oliver's grip was firm, unshakable. Like he was trying to anchor her to the present—

even as the past was crashing over them. Her fingers curled against his shirt, voice hoarse and small.

"I didn't mean to find it."

Oliver exhaled, pressing his cheek against the top of her head.

"I know."

Maggie swallowed hard. "I thought... I thought I'd forgotten it was here."

Oliver's arms tightened.

"I didn't."

Maggie froze. Because something about the way he said it—the certainty, the weight— Made her realize something. Something she should have known all along. She lifted her head, looking at him fully now.

"Do you think about it?"

Oliver's jaw tightened. And then—softly, painfully—

"Every day."

Maggie's breath caught. Because all this time—she thought she had been grieving alone. Thought Oliver had moved on faster. Thought he had let go of something she had never been able to.

But she had been wrong. So very wrong. Because Oliver had never let go. He had just carried it differently.

Maggie looked down at the tiny shoes, her voice barely above a whisper.

"Why didn't we ever talk about it?"

Oliver exhaled slowly.

And then—finally—

"Because I was afraid if I said it out loud, I'd lose you, too."

Maggie stilled. Because suddenly—it all made sense. The distance. The unspoken weight between them. The reason Oliver had pulled back when she thought he had just stopped trying.

She had thought they had grown apart because they had stopped loving each other. But maybe—they had just been too afraid to break under the weight of it. And Maggie was so tired of being afraid.

She shifted in his arms, wrapping her own around him for the first time in years. And Oliver—he let her. His breath stuttered, but he held her tighter.

Because this wasn't just grief anymore. This was acknowledging that they had both been carrying it alone. And finally—they weren't anymore. Maggie pressed her forehead against his shoulder, exhaling shakily.

"We should've talked about it."

Oliver swallowed hard. "Yeah."

Maggie closed her eyes.

"Can we talk about it now?"

Oliver nodded. Without hesitation this time.

"Yeah, Mags."

And just like that—something inside her cracked open. Because for the first time in years—she wasn't holding this alone. And neither was he.

Chapter 33: The Truth She Never Knew

Maggie wasn't sure how long they sat there. Wrapped in something so heavy yet so light. She should have felt drained. She should have felt tired.

Instead—she felt relief. Because for the first time—they weren't running from it. For the first time—they were here. Together.

Eventually, Oliver shifted. Not to pull away. Just to see her. To really see her.

Maggie exhaled. "I don't want to forget."

Oliver shook his head.

"Me neither."

A beat of silence.

Then, softly—"But I don't want it to keep us stuck either."

Maggie swallowed hard.

Because that was the part she hadn't figured out yet. How to let go of the pain without letting go of the love. But maybe—they could figure that out together.

Later that evening, Maggie got another text from Gina.

Gina: Drinks. No excuses. Bring Oliver.

Maggie sighed. Because of course. She had barely responded when Oliver walked in.

Maggie lifted an eyebrow. "Feel like going out?"

Oliver tilted his head. "With?"

Maggie smirked. "The usual troublemakers."

Oliver smirked back. "Gina and Jake?"

Maggie nodded. Oliver sighed, rubbing the back of his neck.

"Are they gonna grill us?"

Maggie pretended to think.

"Oh, absolutely."

Oliver chuckled. "Figured."

Then—softer.

"But we're going anyway?"

Maggie shrugged.

"Yeah. I think we are."

Because suddenly—she didn't feel like hiding anymore. And maybe—that mattered.

The bar was the same as always. But Maggie wasn't. For the first time—she walked in with Oliver, not beside him but with him.

And Gina noticed immediately. She said nothing—at first. Just grinned knowingly as Maggie slid into her seat.

Jake raised a brow. "So, this is happening."

Oliver smirked. "It appears so."

Gina leaned forward.

"Alright. Spill. What changed?"

Maggie's stomach should have clenched. She should have hesitated. But instead—she met Gina's gaze and told her the truth.

"We stopped pretending we were okay."

Gina's grin softened.

Jake nodded. "That's a good start."

Oliver exhaled, settling into his chair. And for the first time—this felt real. Like a beginning.

It happened casually. A passing remark. Something Jake probably didn't even think twice about.

But Maggie heard it. Jake leaned back, glancing at Oliver.

"So, you gonna tell her?"

Oliver froze.

Maggie frowned. "Tell me what?"

Oliver shot Jake a sharp look. Jake winced.

"Sorry. I assumed she knew."

Maggie's stomach twisted.

"Knew what?"

Oliver sighed. Shook his head. But Gina? Gina had that look. Like she had just put the pieces together. And suddenly—Maggie wanted to know.

"Oliver."

Oliver exhaled. Ran a hand down his face. Then—finally—

"Mags... I didn't take the promotion."

Maggie stilled. Because no. That wasn't right. He had—he had gotten an offer. A big one. One that would have moved him to New York.

And she had never stopped him. Had never asked him to stay. Because she had thought—he didn't. But now? Now, Oliver was looking at her like she had missed something huge.

Like this wasn't new information to him. Like this had been his truth all along.

Chapter 34: The Truth She Never Saw

Maggie felt like the ground had just shifted beneath her feet. Like she was looking at Oliver for the first time—and seeing someone she didn't quite recognize.

Because this changed everything. The nights she spent wondering if he even cared anymore. The years she spent believing she was the only one who sacrificed something.

The quiet moments where she thought she had been alone in this. She wasn't. She never had been.

Oliver sighed, rubbing his hands over his face.

"Mags..."

Maggie held up a hand.

"Don't."

Oliver's jaw tightened.

"Just—let me explain."

Maggie's stomach twisted.

"You don't have to explain."

Because she was already piecing it together. The late nights. The stress he had never put words to. The way he had always seemed just a little more tired than he should have been.

She had never questioned it. Had never realized. And now—she wasn't sure how to feel.

Jake cleared his throat. "Uh, so… we're just gonna—"

Gina smacked him. "Shut up, Jake."

Jake muttered, "Yep. Shutting up."

Maggie wasn't paying attention to them anymore. Because Oliver was watching her. Waiting. Like he knew this was the moment she would either lean in or walk away. And for once—Maggie didn't know which one she was about to do.

Maggie swallowed hard.

"You had an offer."

Oliver nodded. "Yeah."

Maggie blinked.

"And you turned it down."

Another nod. "Yeah."

Maggie's heart pounded.

"But why?"

Oliver exhaled.

Then—softer.

"Because I couldn't leave you, Mags."

Maggie stilled. Because there it was. The truth she had never even considered. He had stayed. He had always stayed. And all this time—she had never known.

Maggie's breath was uneven. Her mind was racing.

"But I—I never asked you to stay."

Oliver's lips pressed into a thin line.

"No. You didn't."

Maggie's throat tightened.

"You should have told me."

Oliver's gaze was steady.

"Would it have changed anything?"

Maggie opened her mouth—but she didn't have an answer. Because would it have? Would she have told him to go? Would she have felt more guilty? Would she have resented him sooner? She didn't know. And that terrified her. Maggie swallowed against the lump in her throat.

"All this time, I thought..."

Oliver's brows pulled together. "Thought what?"

Maggie let out a breath that felt too heavy.

"I thought I was the only one who gave up something."

Oliver exhaled slowly.

"I know."

Maggie winced. Because he had let her believe that. For years. For much too long. And now—it hurt in a way she hadn't expected.

She stood up. Too fast. Her chair scraped loudly against the floor, making Gina flinch. Oliver was already moving.

"Maggie—"

But she shook her head.

"I need a second."

Oliver's jaw tightened, but he didn't push. Didn't chase her.

He just nodded. "Okay."

Maggie turned and walked out the door. Because suddenly—she needed air. Because suddenly—this was too much. And because suddenly—she wasn't sure how to breathe.

Chapter 35: The Weight of Knowing

Maggie's hands shook as she stepped outside. The night air was cooler than she expected. She hadn't even grabbed her jacket. Hadn't thought about it. Because all she could think about—was Oliver. And the fact that he had given up everything for her. And she had never known.

She paced near the sidewalk, trying to steady her breath. But her mind was a storm. Why hadn't he told her? Why had he let her believe he didn't care? Why had he stayed if he was just going to let them fall apart?

Her chest tightened. Because it wasn't that simple, was it? Oliver had stayed. But he had also kept his distance. Because maybe—he had thought he was protecting her.

Maybe—he had been protecting himself, too. And now? Now Maggie had to figure out what to do with that.

She heard the door swing open. Footsteps behind her. And she didn't have to turn to know—it was him. Oliver stepped beside her, hands shoved in his pockets. They stood there for a second. Not speaking. Just existing in the same space. Then—softly.

"I'm sorry you found out like that."

Maggie exhaled. She wasn't mad. Not really. She was just—raw. She turned to him, her voice barely above a whisper.

"Why didn't you tell me?"

Oliver held her gaze. Then—with quiet honesty.

"Because I didn't want you to feel trapped."

Maggie's stomach dropped. Because he really believed that, didn't he? He had stayed. But he had also given her space. Because he thought that's what she needed. And maybe—that had been their biggest mistake. They had both been waiting for the other person to close the distance. And neither of them had. Until now.

Maggie inhaled deeply. Then—without hesitation—she reached for his hand. Oliver's breath hitched. Like he hadn't been expecting that. Like he still wasn't sure if she wanted him to hold on. But Maggie? She wanted him to. So she squeezed. Tight. And finally—Oliver squeezed back. Maggie swallowed hard, staring at their hands.

"I didn't know," she admitted.

Oliver nodded.

"I know."

A beat of silence.

Then, softly—"Would it have changed anything?"

Maggie exhaled.

And this time—she had an answer.

"Yes."

Because maybe—if she had known, she wouldn't have felt so alone. Maybe—if she had known, she would have fought harder. Maybe—if she had known, she wouldn't have spent so long believing they had already lost. And Oliver just nodded. Because maybe—he had always hoped that would be her answer.

Maggie wasn't done thinking. She wasn't done processing. But there was one thing she did know. She wasn't going to let this be another moment that passed them by. She looked up at him, her fingers still curled in his.

"Can we go home?"

Oliver stilled.

Then—his entire face softened.

"Yeah, Mags."

And just like that—they walked home together. Not in silence. Not with distance. But with something that finally felt like a beginning.

Chapter 36: Choosing Him Back

Maggie hadn't expected clarity. Not yet. But when she woke the next morning—something was different. She still had questions. Still had a thousand emotions pulling at her. But there was one thing she knew. She didn't want Oliver to be the only one trying. She wanted to choose him back.

Oliver was already in the kitchen when Maggie walked in. Like always. Like before. Like things hadn't changed—but they had.

He glanced up, expecting hesitation. But this time—Maggie didn't hesitate. She stepped forward and poured herself coffee. And then—without thinking, without overanalyzing— She set a second mug in front of Oliver.

Oliver stilled. Not because of the coffee. But because it was the first time in a long time she had done something just for him. Maggie met his gaze.

"I don't want you to be the only one making an effort."

Oliver blinked. Once. Twice. Then—his expression softened. And Maggie finally felt like they were in this together.

Later that day, Maggie found herself standing in the spare room. The one Oliver had turned into a storage space. The one filled with forgotten things.

Her eyes landed on something in the corner. Something covered in a dusted-over sheet. She knew what it was before she even touched it. She pulled the sheet back—and there it was.

The old guitar. The one Oliver had bought years ago. The one he had dreamed of fixing up, back when they still talked about the future.

Maggie's chest tightened. Because he never did. Because somewhere along the way—he stopped believing he had time. Or maybe—he stopped believing he deserved to. She wasn't sure when that had happened. But she knew one thing for certain. She was going to fix it.

She didn't tell Oliver. Not yet. She just made some calls. Found someone who could help her restore it. Because this wasn't just about the guitar. It was about everything Oliver had given up without saying a word. And maybe—if she did this for him—he would finally see what she saw. That he was worth the effort, too.

That evening, Oliver found her in the living room. Maggie looked up from her sketchbook.

He hesitated. "What are you drawing?"

Maggie smirked. "Wouldn't you like to know?"

Oliver raised a brow. Then—he surprised her. He sat down beside her. Close. Not touching—but close enough that she could feel the warmth of him.

She let him. Because for the first time in *years*—she wasn't afraid of getting too close. Because *this time*—she wasn't planning on pulling away.

Chapter 37: The Things Left Unsaid

Maggie had always been good at fixing things. At rearranging. At smoothing over edges. At making things whole again. But this? This wasn't just fixing something broken. This was giving something back. To Oliver. To the boy she had fallen in love with. To the man who had stayed. Even when she hadn't known it.

Maggie sat in her car, gripping the steering wheel. The guitar was in the backseat. Restored. Better than new. It had taken weeks. More phone calls than she cared to count. A trip out of town to find the right parts. And now—it was done.

Her stomach twisted. Because this was it. This was her telling Oliver—I see you. This was her saying—I'm choosing you, too.

And that was terrifying. But she wasn't going to run from it. Not anymore.

Oliver was in the kitchen when she walked in. Because of course he was. She had learned that about him. That he always ended up here. Like this space was safe. Like it was the one place he knew how to exist.

Maggie exhaled. "I have something for you."

Oliver froze. Then—slowly—he turned. Maggie held up the case.

Oliver blinked. "What is that?"

Maggie swallowed hard. And then—she handed it to him. Oliver hesitated. Then, carefully—he unlatched the case.

His breath hitched. Because there it was. The guitar. *His* guitar. Only—it wasn't the same. It was whole again. Beautiful.

Maggie's voice was quiet.

"I thought you should have it back."

Oliver just stared. Not at the guitar. At her. Like he wasn't sure what to do with this. With her. With the fact that Maggie had done this. For him.

Maggie shifted.

"I know you gave things up for me."

Oliver exhaled sharply. Maggie bit her lip.

"And I know I didn't see it. Not really."

Oliver's jaw tightened.

"Maggie—"

But she shook her head.

"Let me say this."

Oliver nodded. Maggie took a breath.

"I spent so long thinking I was the only one who sacrificed something."

She swallowed hard.

"But I wasn't."

Oliver looked away. Like maybe—this was too much. But Maggie She was done hiding from the truth. So she stepped forward. And—softly, carefully—she reached for his hand. Oliver stilled. Maggie's fingers tightened around his.

"I see you, Oliver."

Oliver's breath shuddered. Maggie lifted her chin.

"I see everything you did. Everything you gave up."

A beat of silence. Then—softer.

"And I want you to have something back."

Oliver's fingers clenched around hers. Like maybe—this was undoing him. Like maybe—he had waited years to hear this.

And Maggie wasn't going anywhere.

Oliver finally looked up. His expression was carefully unreadable. But his voice? Not so much.

"Why now?"

Maggie exhaled. Then—softly.

"Because I finally see what I should have seen all along."

Oliver's jaw tightened.

And she stepped closer.

"You stayed, Oliver."

A breath.

"And I want you to know—I would've stayed, too."

Oliver's breath hitched. And just like that—Maggie knew that this moment was everything. Because this wasn't just about a guitar. It was about them. And finally, finally—Oliver saw that, too.

Chapter 38: The Weight of Being Seen

Oliver didn't know how to hold this moment. Didn't know how to breathe through it. Because Maggie had just done something he never saw coming.

She had handed him a piece of himself—one he thought was gone. And now, he was standing in their kitchen, holding a guitar that had once been forgotten. Holding proof that Maggie had been paying attention. That she saw him. And that? That was almost too much.

Maggie stood quietly, watching him. Like she was waiting. Like she knew this was a lot. Like she was giving him space to process it. Oliver exhaled. Ran a hand over the strings. It had been so long.

He swallowed hard. "Mags..."

Maggie tilted her head. And Oliver didn't have the words. Not yet. So instead—he just looked at her. Like maybe—this was undoing him. Because maybe—it was. Maggie didn't push. Didn't ask him to talk. She just... let it be.

That night, Oliver sat on the couch with the guitar. Didn't play it. Just held it. Like he was trying to remember who he used to be.

Maggie didn't say a word. She just curled up at the other end of the couch. Not touching. But close enough that he knew she was there.

And for the first time *in a long time*—Oliver let himself sit in that. Let himself believe that she meant it. That she wanted to be here. With him.

The next morning, Maggie found Oliver in the kitchen. Only—he wasn't just making coffee. He was holding the guitar. His fingers curled over the strings. Like he had been sitting with something all night.

Maggie hesitated.

"Are you gonna play it?"

Oliver exhaled.

Then—softly.

"I don't know if I remember how."

Maggie tilted her head.

"Would it be so bad to try?"

Oliver looked at her then. Really looked. And Maggie saw it. Saw the hesitation. Saw the fear of getting it wrong. Saw the way he wasn't just talking about the guitar anymore.

And Maggie wasn't going to let him stay in that place. So—she made the choice for him. She reached out. Soft. Careful. And she traced her fingers over his. Guiding them to the first chord.

Oliver's breath hitched. Maggie swallowed hard.

"Start here."

And just like that—Oliver played the first note. The first sound. The first step toward something he thought he had lost. And maybe—that was everything.

Chapter 39: A Different Kind of Beginning

Oliver hadn't meant to let his guard down. Hadn't meant to let Maggie in this far. But she was already here. Already woven back into places he didn't realize he had been keeping her out of. And now—he wasn't sure how to keep pretending he didn't want her here.

The sound of the guitar still lingered in the air. Soft. Unpolished. But real. Maggie hadn't said anything when he started playing. Hadn't made a big deal out of it. She had just stayed. Had just watched.

Like she had been waiting for this moment longer than he had. And Oliver? He wasn't used to that. Wasn't used to being the one on the receiving end of a grand gesture. And now he didn't know what to do with it.

Later that night, Maggie was in the bedroom. Not asleep. Not pretending to be. Just sitting against the headboard, sketchbook balanced on her lap.

Oliver hesitated in the doorway. Because this was different. He had been taking the guest room. Taking space. But tonight—Maggie hadn't closed the door.

Tonight—he didn't want to take space. Not from her. Not anymore.

So—he did something he hadn't done in a long time. He stepped inside.

And Maggie? She looked up. Her breath caught. Not because she was surprised. But because she wasn't. That was all the permission he needed.

Oliver crossed the room. Slow. Measured. Like he was giving her a chance to change her mind. Like he was giving himself a chance to change his.

Maggie didn't move. Didn't tense. Didn't pull away. She just watched him. Waited for him. And when Oliver reached the edge of the bed—she shifted. Made space. Not because she had to. But because she wanted to. And Oliver finally let himself believe that.

He sat down. Not too close. Not too far. Just close enough. Close enough to feel the warmth of her body next to his. Close enough to remember what this used to feel like. Close enough to want more. Maggie exhaled. Then—softer.

"You don't have to sleep in the guest room."

Oliver's breath hitched. Maggie swallowed hard.

"I mean, if you still want to, that's fine. I just…"

She hesitated. Then—quieter.

"I don't think I want you to."

Oliver stared at her. She held his gaze. Didn't backtrack. Didn't take it back. She had made a choice.

He wasn't going to run from that. So—he made his own. He reached for the blanket. And just like that—he stayed.

Chapter 40: The Morning After Feels Different

Oliver woke to warmth. To Maggie. Her back pressed against his chest. His arm resting around her waist. Like they had never stopped sleeping like this. Only—they had. And now—it was real again.

Oliver didn't know how long he stayed still. Didn't know how long he let himself breathe her in. Because part of him was afraid. Afraid of breaking the moment. Afraid of what came next. But then—Maggie stirred. And Oliver didn't move away.

Maggie stretched just slightly. And then—she exhaled. Soft. Content. Like she hadn't slept this well in years. Oliver felt something in his chest pull tight. Because he knew the feeling. Then—her voice, still drowsy.

"You're awake."

Oliver smirked against her shoulder.

"So are you."

Maggie hummed. Didn't move.

"Don't say anything stupid to ruin this."

Oliver chuckled.

"I'd never."

Maggie laughed—a soft, sleepy sound. And just like that—Oliver felt himself exhale. Because this wasn't complicated. This was just them.

Eventually, Maggie rolled over. Faced him fully. Her fingers traced absent circles against his chest. Oliver let her. Let himself lean into her touch. Then—softly.

"What happens now?"

Oliver didn't hesitate.

"We keep going."

Maggie tilted her head.

"And if it gets hard again?"

Oliver held her gaze.

"Then we don't run from it this time."

Maggie's breath hitched. Because he meant it. Because this time—they weren't going to let each other go.

Chapter 41: The Choice to Keep Choosing

Maggie had always thought waking up next to someone should feel natural. Like muscle memory. Like breathing. Like something you didn't have to think about.

But this? This was different. Because this wasn't just waking up next to Oliver. This was waking up next to him after everything. And that made all the difference.

Oliver was already awake. Not watching her—but close. Like he had been waiting for her to be the first one to move. Maggie blinked up at him. And then—softly.

"Hey."

Oliver smirked. "Hey."

Maggie exhaled. It should have felt awkward. It should have felt like too much. But instead—it just felt easy. Oliver stretched, sighing.

"So, do we just pretend last night didn't happen?"

Maggie raised an eyebrow.

"Do you want to pretend?"

Oliver grinned.

"Nope."

And Maggie? She laughed. Because of course this was how he'd handle it. And maybe—that was exactly what she needed.

Maggie sat up. Ran a hand through her hair. Then—glanced at Oliver.

"So, what do we do now?"

Oliver smirked.

"I was thinking breakfast."

Maggie rolled her eyes. "Obviously."

Oliver chuckled.

But then—his expression softened.

"No, but really, Mags. We just… keep going."

Maggie held his gaze. Because that was it, wasn't it? There was no big dramatic answer. No grand declaration. It was just choosing each other. Over and over.

And she could do that. So she smiled.

"Okay."

The smell of coffee filled the kitchen. Maggie leaned against the counter, watching Oliver move. It was strange. How normal it all felt. How easy. And maybe—that was the best part. Because this wasn't about forcing anything. This was just them. And maybe— that was enough. For now. For always.

Chapter 42: The Space Between Old and New

Maggie wasn't sure what she expected. For everything to feel brand new? For it to feel like nothing had changed? For there to be some clear, defining moment where she just knew everything was different?

But instead—it was something in between. A mix of old habits and new choices. A slow shift. Not a restart. But a continuation. Something that had never truly ended—just paused.

Oliver was still the one making coffee. Maggie was still the one waiting for the first sip to kick in before speaking. But now? Now Oliver slid a mug toward her without needing to ask how she wanted it.

Maggie made toast and actually waited for him to sit down before eating. Because this wasn't just breakfast. This was them. Choosing to sit together. Choosing to be in the same space. Choosing not to rush away from it.

By the time they both had to leave for work, Maggie realized something. They were moving through the morning like they always had. But it wasn't quite the same. Because there were moments—small ones—that felt different.

The way Oliver brushed past her in the hallway just a little too slowly. The way Maggie lingered just a second longer when their hands touched reaching for the same thing. The way Oliver opened the door for her as they both stepped outside. Like he wasn't ready to stop being near her yet. And Maggie wasn't, either.

Midday, Maggie's phone buzzed. A text. From Oliver.

Oliver: How's your day going?

Maggie stared at the screen. Because this was different. Oliver wasn't someone who sent random check-ins. Not because he didn't care. But because it just wasn't him. She hesitated. Then—softly smiling—she typed back.

Maggie: Better now. You?

The response came almost immediately.

Oliver: Same.

And Maggie's chest tightened. Because this was what had been missing before. Not just the big things. But the little things. The small moments that reminded them they were still thinking about each other—even when they weren't in the same room.

And now? Now, Oliver was making the effort. And Maggie was letting herself believe it. That night, Maggie found herself in the spare room. The one Oliver had turned into storage over the years. The guitar case was still there, propped against the wall.

She ran her fingers along the edge. And just like that—a thought settled in her chest. She wasn't the only one with dreams that had been pushed aside.

Oliver had made sacrifices, too. And Maggie wasn't done giving something back. Not yet.

Chapter 43: Giving Back

Maggie had never been the kind of person who needed grand gestures. She wasn't looking for extravagant displays of affection. Didn't need some dramatic proclamation of love. But this was something else.

Because this was about Oliver. About giving him something he didn't even realize he deserved. Something he had given her without hesitation—years ago. Something she should have seen sooner.

Maggie stood in the spare room, fingertips grazing the edge of the guitar case. It wasn't just about the music. Not really. It was about what it represented.

About the boy Oliver used to be—the man he had become—the sacrifices he had made. Maggie had always thought she was the only one who had lost something. But Oliver had been losing things, too. Piece by piece. And Maggie wasn't going to let him lose himself anymore.

That evening, Maggie found Oliver in the kitchen. Because of course he was there. She leaned against the doorway, watching him. For a moment, she just stood there.

Because there was something about this. The way he moved around the space so naturally. The way he didn't need to be told how she took her tea or what mug she preferred. The way he had never stopped showing up. And maybe—Maggie was just now starting to understand what that meant. Oliver looked up. Smirked.

"I can feel you staring at me."

Maggie huffed a laugh.

"Maybe I like looking at you."

Oliver's brows lifted. Maggie rolled her eyes.

"Don't let it go to your head."

Oliver grinned.

"Too late."

Maggie shook her head—but the warmth in her chest stayed. And suddenly—she knew what she needed to do.

Maggie took a slow breath. Then—carefully.

"I want to take you somewhere."

Oliver blinked.

"Right now?"

Maggie smirked.

"No, tomorrow."

Oliver narrowed his eyes.

"This isn't some elaborate plan to get me into a suit, is it?"

Maggie laughed.

"Absolutely not."

Oliver studied her. And then—something shifted in his expression. Like he knew this was something more. Like he knew she wasn't just asking him to humor her. And finally—softly.

"Okay, Mags."

Maggie exhaled. Because he said yes. Because he was trusting her. And maybe—that was the most important part.

Maggie sat in bed that night, staring at her phone. At the confirmation email. At the choice she had made for Oliver. She didn't know if he would love it. Didn't know if he would resist it. Didn't know if he was ready for it. But she knew one thing. He deserved this. Deserved to take back a part of himself. And tomorrow—he would. Even if he didn't know it yet.

Chapter 44: The Gift He Didn't Ask For

Oliver didn't like surprises. Never had. He liked predictability. Liked knowing what was coming next. Liked being in control of the outcome. So, naturally—Maggie refused to tell him where they were going. Which meant he spent the entire drive trying to guess.

Oliver glanced at her from the passenger seat.

"Are we going to one of those paint-and-sip things?"

Maggie huffed a laugh.

"Absolutely not."

Oliver smirked.

"You sure? You seemed to enjoy dragging me to one that one time."

Maggie shrugged.

"You looked good in an apron."

Oliver snorted.

"Okay, but seriously—where are we going?"

Maggie just grinned.

"You'll see."

Oliver sighed dramatically.

"Not sure I like this new, mysterious side of you."

Maggie smirked.

"Yes, you do."

And Oliver?

Yeah. He really, really did.

Oliver realized exactly what was happening the second she pulled into the parking lot. His entire body went still. Maggie put the car in park, watching him carefully. Waiting for him to say something. Waiting for him to react. Oliver exhaled.

"Is this…?"

Maggie nodded.

"It is."

Oliver blinked. Stared at the music studio in front of them. Then back at Maggie.

"Why?"

Maggie's expression softened.

"Because you deserve this."

Oliver swallowed hard. Because he wasn't sure he did.

Oliver had forgotten what it felt like to want something for himself. To even think about the possibility. Music had been something he let go of a long time ago. Not because he didn't love it. But because life happened. Because work was practical. Because bills needed to be paid. Because dreams didn't always make the cut.

And now—Maggie was handing him a piece of that back. Like it was nothing. Like it was everything. Oliver exhaled.

"Maggie..."

Maggie reached for his hand.

"Just try it, Oliver. That's all I'm asking."

Oliver looked at her. Saw how much she meant it. Saw how much she wanted this—for him. And that? That was enough. So he nodded. And together—they stepped inside.

Chapter 45: The Sound of Something Coming Back

Oliver didn't know how to step into this. Didn't know how to let himself want this. But now? Now he was here. Standing in a music studio. With Maggie. And the weight of it was heavier than he expected.

Maggie had set this up. Arranged everything. There was already a guitar waiting for him. Already a quiet expectation in the air. But Oliver? He wasn't sure he could do this. Because it had been years.

Years since he had picked up a guitar for himself. Years since he had played just to play. Years since he had let himself be this guy. And now? Now, he wasn't sure if that guy even existed anymore.

Maggie sat across from him. Didn't say a word. Didn't push. She just... waited. Like she knew he had to be the one to make the first move. Like she knew this wasn't about the music. This was about him.

Oliver exhaled slowly. Ran his fingers over the guitar strings. And the second he did—something shifted. Because it wasn't gone. Not completely. It was still there. Buried, but waiting. And Oliver? He wasn't sure what to do with that.

The first note was hesitant. Soft. Careful. The second came a little easier. And then—the rest followed. Maggie smiled. Not because he was perfect. But because he was trying. And for the first time in a long time—Oliver didn't want to stop.

By the time he put the guitar down, something was different. Not just with the music. With him. Because he had spent so long believing this part of himself was gone. Had spent so long convincing himself it didn't matter.

But now? Now he wasn't so sure. Because Maggie had given him more than just music back. She had given him the chance to believe in it again. And that was everything.

Maggie reached for his hand. Not as a reward. Not as a congratulation. Just as a reminder. That she was here. That she was in this with him. That he didn't have to figure it all out alone. For the first time in years—he let himself believe that.

Chapter 46: Bringing It Home

Oliver hadn't expected to feel different. Not right away. But as they drove home, something sat differently in his chest. Not just because he had played. Not just because he had let himself want something again. But because Maggie had seen him. Had believed in him—when he hadn't believed in himself. And that was new.

Maggie didn't fill the silence. Didn't try to make him talk about it. She just… let him sit with it.

Oliver wasn't used to that. Wasn't used to someone understanding that sometimes, silence was the only way to process. So, instead of forcing a conversation—he just reached for her hand. And Maggie didn't hesitate.

By the time they pulled into the driveway, something had settled. Not in a bad way. Not in a way that felt like pressure. But in a way that felt… good.

Like they had taken a real step forward. Like this wasn't just some fragile thing waiting to break. Oliver followed Maggie inside. Watched as she kicked off her shoes, stretching like she hadn't been sitting for an hour. And then—her voice, soft.

"You okay?"

Oliver blinked. Because, honestly? Yeah. For the first time in a long time, he was. So he nodded.

"Yeah, Mags. I think I am."

Maggie's smile was small. Real. And Oliver didn't overthink it. He just pulled her in. Held her there.

Because for the first time *in years*—this felt like home again.

They didn't rush anything. Didn't feel the need to fill the space with more words than necessary. Maggie made tea. Oliver found himself picking up the guitar again—just to feel the weight of it in his hands.

And when it was time for bed? Maggie didn't have to ask him to stay. Because Oliver was already planning on it.

As they settled under the covers, Maggie turned toward him. Watched him. Like she was still figuring out what to say. Oliver smirked.

"Don't say anything stupid to ruin this."

Maggie laughed. Then—softly.

"I wasn't going to."

Oliver raised an eyebrow. Maggie sighed dramatically.

"Okay, maybe I was."

Oliver chuckled. Then—before she could overthink it—he reached for her. Pulled her against his chest. Held her. And Maggie did more than just let him, she moved in closer. Because they weren't just choosing each other now. They were choosing each other tomorrow. And maybe—for every day after that.

Chapter 47: The Second Surprise

Maggie hadn't planned on doing this so soon. Hadn't planned on pushing forward before Oliver had fully settled into the first surprise. But the moment felt right.

Because Oliver wasn't just going through the motions anymore. He was here. Present. And Maggie wanted to keep giving him back pieces of himself. Even if he didn't know he was ready for them yet.

Maggie had been thinking about this for weeks. Had almost talked herself out of it a dozen times. Because what if it was too much, too soon? What if Oliver wasn't ready to face it?

What if he thought she was trying to fix him instead of just... giving back what was already his? But now? Now, watching him sit at the kitchen table, casually running his fingers over the guitar strings— She knew. She knew it was time.

Oliver looked up when she entered the room. Raising a brow at the way she was standing there, clearly up to something. Maggie smirked.

"You don't trust me at all, do you?"

Oliver set the guitar down, leaning back in his chair.

"I trust you."

A beat.

"But I also know that look."

Maggie laughed.

Because of course he did. She moved to the closet in the hallway, pulling out a case. Not a guitar case. Something smaller. Something Oliver hadn't seen in years.

She turned—holding it out to him. And Oliver's entire body went still. Because he knew what this was.

Oliver didn't move at first. Didn't reach for it. Didn't say anything. Because how? How had she found it? Maggie's voice was soft.

"I kept it."

Oliver exhaled sharply. Finally, slowly, carefully—he took the case from her hands. His fingers traced over the edges. Because he remembered this. It was his first harmonica. The one he had carried everywhere as a teenager.

The one he had played absentmindedly when he wasn't sure how to say what he was feeling. The one he had stopped playing when life got in the way. And Maggie had kept it.

Oliver swallowed hard. Then—without thinking—he opened the case. It was worn, but perfect. Like it had been waiting for him. He let his fingers hover over it. Then—before he could stop himself—he picked it up.

Maggie watched. Didn't speak. Didn't push. Just... waited.

For the first time *in years*—Oliver lifted it to his lips. And played.

The first note was soft. Rusty. But it was there. It was him. And Maggie smiled. Because this wasn't just about music. This was about Oliver remembering who he used to be. About showing him that he had never really lost it.

And when Oliver looked at her—eyes ju*st a little too bright*—he didn't have to say anything.

Because Maggie already knew. She just stepped forward. And wrapped her arms around him. Because he had always done this for her. And now—it was her turn.

Chapter 48: The Conversation That Needed to Happen

Oliver hadn't planned on talking about the future tonight. Hadn't planned on laying everything out like this. But maybe—that was the point. Because Maggie had just given him a part of himself back. And Oliver wasn't going to let that go without giving something back to her, too.

They were still in the kitchen. Still sitting across from each other. The harmonica was on the table between them. Like a silent reminder. A reminder that they weren't the same people they used to be.

That they had both lost things along the way. That maybe—this wasn't just about finding each other again. Maybe—this was about finding themselves, too. Maggie exhaled.

"So... what now?"

Oliver leaned back in his chair. Smirked.

"Why do you always ask me that?"

Maggie raised an eyebrow.

"Because you always have an answer."

Oliver huffed a laugh. But then—his expression softened. And for the first time in a long time—he really thought about it.

Oliver ran a hand through his hair. Then—quietly.

"I want to keep doing this."

Maggie tilted her head.

"Doing what?"

Oliver met her gaze.

"Choosing each other."

Maggie's breath hitched. Because that was the answer, wasn't it? Not some big, dramatic plan. Not some perfectly mapped-out future. Just choosing each other. Every day. Maggie swallowed hard. Then—softly.

"Me too."

Oliver smirked.

"Good. Because I already bought you a plane ticket."

Maggie blinked.

"You what?"

Oliver grinned.

"Paris, Mags. We never did it."

Maggie's heart stuttered. Because she knew what he was saying. They had spent so long holding back. So long sacrificing pieces of themselves for what they thought the other needed.

And now Oliver was telling her they didn't have to do that anymore. Now he was giving something back, too. Maggie swallowed hard. Then—smiling softly.

"When do we leave?"

Oliver leaned forward. Rested his forearms on the table. Smirked.

"You tell me."

And Maggie? For the first time in years—she felt like she could.

Chapter 49: One Last Night In Their Old Life

Maggie had forgotten what excitement felt like. Not the kind that came from crossing things off a to-do list. Not the kind that came from momentary distractions. But the kind that felt like possibility. Like something new.

And now? Now she was feeling it again. Because Paris wasn't just about a trip. It was about finally letting themselves live.

Gina and Jake had insisted on a sendoff. Which, in their language, meant drinks at Lupe's. Maggie and Oliver hadn't argued. Because there was something fitting about ending where it all started.

Lupe greeted them with a knowing grin.

"So, you two aren't just pretending anymore?"

Maggie rolled her eyes.

"Guess not."

Lupe chuckled.

"Well, it only took you long enough."

Oliver smirked.

"Appreciate the patience, Lupe."

Lupe waved him off.

"Patience? Please. I just enjoy a good show."

Maggie laughed. Because—of course she did.

Gina plopped onto the barstool next to Maggie. Jake took the seat next to Oliver. And for a moment—it felt just like old times. Like all the complications hadn't happened. Like life hadn't made a mess of things. Gina nudged Maggie's arm.

"So, Paris, huh?"

Maggie nodded. Gina grinned.

"Well, my friend. Took you long enough."

Maggie sighed.

"Why does everyone keep saying that?"

Jake snorted.

"Because it's true."

Oliver smirked.

"Alright, alright, no need to roast us before we even leave."

Gina winked.

"No promises."

And Maggie?

She couldn't stop smiling. Because she had forgotten how much she missed this. Not just Oliver. But the whole crazy mess of them.

Lupe set down four drinks. Jake raised an eyebrow.

"We didn't order yet."

Lupe smirked.

"I know."

Maggie glanced at her drink. Then at Oliver's. Then at Gina's and Jake's. And suddenly—she knew exactly what Lupe had done. Lupe grinned.

"Figured we'd do this right. One last round of 'What If.'"

Maggie's chest tightened. Because it had been so long. Since they had sat here. Since they had asked those stupid, reckless, wonderful questions. Since they had let themselves imagine more.

Oliver lifted his glass. Smirked.

"Alright then. One last 'What If.'"

Maggie hesitated. Then—softly.

"What if this is just the beginning?"

And Oliver? He raised his glass toward hers.

"Then we don't waste another second."

Chapter 50: A Parisian Toast

Maggie and Oliver wandered until the night stretched endlessly. Until the city felt like theirs. Until they found themselves in a quiet little bar—no tourists, no rush, just the soft hum of conversation and the clink of glasses around them.

A place that felt like it had been waiting for them. No plans. No expectations. Just this moment. Oliver ordered a whiskey. Maggie scanned the menu, her lips curving into a soft smile.

"I'll have a Kir Royale."

Oliver lifted a brow.

"Fancy."

Maggie smirked.

"When in France."

Oliver chuckled.

The bartender set their drinks down, and for a moment, neither of them moved. Because this wasn't just another toast. This was something else.

Something bigger.

Maggie lifted her glass first.

"To all the 'What Ifs.'"

Oliver held her gaze. And then—with quiet certainty.

"To finally knowing the answer."

And when they drank—it wasn't just to the past. It was to everything ahead.

Epilogue: The Taste of Forever

Maggie dipped her toes into the warm sand, letting the waves tease at her ankles. The sun hung low in the sky, casting golden ribbons across the water. Somewhere behind her, music drifted through the air—soft, familiar, effortless. And beside her? Oliver. Holding two drinks.

Maggie turned as he handed her one. She didn't have to ask what it was. The moment she caught the scent of coconut and pineapple, she laughed.

"A piña colada?"

Oliver smirked, taking a slow sip of his own.

"You didn't think I'd forget, did you?"

Maggie shook her head.

"No, I suppose I didn't."

Oliver tilted his glass toward her.

"To tradition."

Maggie clinked hers against his.

"To everything that got us here."

And when they drank—it wasn't just nostalgia. It wasn't just a callback. It was a reminder. Of how far they had come. Of how much they had fought for this. Of every single choice that led them here. And Maggie? She wouldn't change a single one.

The ocean breeze tangled through Oliver's hair. He set his drink down, stretching his arms over his head, looking at her with easy familiarity.

"Think we made the right choice?"

Maggie smiled.

Not just with her lips, but with everything in her. The kind of smile you didn't have to think about. The kind of smile that just existed—because it was real.

"Not a single doubt."

Oliver chuckled.

Then—with that same smirk that had always undone her.

"Well, in that case…"

He grabbed her hand.

And before she could even think—he was pulling her into the waves. Maggie shrieked, laughing, fighting it—but not really.

Because this? This was everything.

And Oliver? He was hers.

For now. For always.

The End.

Author's Note

Dear Reader,

I hope you enjoyed reading this story as much as I enjoyed writing it. For a long time, I've had a soft spot for *Escape (The Piña Colada Song)* by Rupert Holmes—it's one of my guilty pleasures.

At first, I wrote this story purely for my own entertainment, but as it came together, I realized I couldn't just keep it to myself. That's one of the joys of being an indie author—I get to explore different genres and follow wherever inspiration takes me. Since my mind is always brimming with ideas, I often find myself working on multiple stories at once. That's probably why this is already my third release in just six weeks!

New releases—especially from indie authors—always need a little extra support. If you enjoyed this story (or any of my previous books), I would truly appreciate it if you left an honest review on the platform where you purchased or downloaded it, or on Goodreads. Your review not only helps other readers decide whether to pick up my book but also makes a huge difference in helping my work reach a wider audience.

Thank you for reading, and I hope to share more stories with you soon!

Best,

Zoey Michaels

Previous Releases and Future Projects

Released in 2025

The Seventh Minute	*Contemporary Fantasy*
The Echoed Mind	*Dystopian/Cyberpunk*
Love, Lies, and Pina Coladas	*Romance*

Upcoming Projects

The Eighth Minute	*Contemporary Fantasy*
Angry Air	*Fantasy/Dystopian*
The Prescribed Lie	*Dystopian/Futuristic*
(Book 1: The Pharmacracy Series)	
The Breaking Point	*Psychological Thriller*

For the latest news, previews and updates visit ZoeyMichaels.com or follow me on Facebook

www.ingramcontent.com/pod-product-compliance
Lightning Source LLC
Chambersburg PA
CBHW071220260626
47162CB00004B/1373